INSURGENTS

HARMONY SERIES BOOK ONE

INSURGENTS

MARGARET BALL

**Galway
Publishing**

Copyright © 2017 Margaret Ball

Published by Galway Publishing

ISBN Paperback: 978-1-947648-02-9
ISBN eBook: 978-1-947648-03-6

Printed in the United States of America

Cover and Interior Design: Ghislain Viau
Cover Art: Bogdan Maksimovic

For Steve, my First Reader, who doesn't even like science fiction but reads my manuscripts anyway.

PROLOGUE

The age of space exploration did not start immediately after the discovery of wormholes that connected far distant parts of the galaxy. It started a generation later, after physicists and engineers figured out how to build a very small spaceship that would not be torn apart by the unpredictable fluctuations of spacetime around wormholes.

The age of colonization was yet another generation distant; it took that long to develop ships large enough to withstand the assault on their geometry that occurred at wormholes.

Harmony Colony was one of the earliest settlements, founded by a group of idealists who wanted to build a new society without any of the bigotry or greed or hate of the world they were leaving behind. There was no shortage of volunteers; four colony ships were required just to transport the starter population.

Over the generations, the continuing battle against anti-social thinking bred a number of obdurate citizens who refused to conform to the standards of Harmony. Fortunately there existed a second continent, uninviting to the original settlers, to which these criminals could be deported. Harmony named this land the Penal Colony; the deportees called it Esilia, the land of exiles.

After generations of sending anyone who had issues with the central government, Harmony should not have been surprised when Esilians decided they wanted to be independent of the homeland and its taxes.

CHAPTER ONE

"Do I have to spell it out? You. Are. Not. Going." Jesse glowered at the younger and slighter man who stood casually leaning on a needle tree at the edge of the clearing.

"Maybe I'm the one who should spell it out. I. Am. Your. Captain. And I do not send my men out into danger that I don't share." Gabrel Moresco folded his arms and returned Jesse's glare.

"Ha! Captain? Just because Travis sprinkled commissions around like Festival candy doesn't mean you outrank me."

"Actually, Jesse, it does."

"As your medic, I'm reporting you to yourself as not fit for duty. If you hadn't taken a dive into that ravine—"

"I'd be terminally unfit for duty, with a burn from a blaster that was cranked up to maximum. I'd probably be *melted*. Did you see what happened to the olive tree?"

"But you did leap into the ravine, and unlike the native animals you don't have four little hooves to help you balance, and you went down and twisted your knee so badly we had to drag you out of there."

"I would have been fine! Only there was this round rock... it turned underfoot. Could have happened to anybody."

"Doesn't matter how it happened. The fact is that you can't put your weight on that leg without gasping. You've probably pulled a tendon. You're a liability to any raiding party. Hell, you can't even hobble down the mountain to where the float is waiting."

"So strap it tighter."

"Bind it any tighter and I'll cut off your circulation. Stand down, Gabrel. This is not your party."

"It was *my idea!*" But Gabrel shut up. Jesse was right and he knew it; a man who couldn't run had no business on a raid. Even a supposedly peaceful mission like the one he'd planned had the potential to go south at any moment. He'd be putting the others in even more danger if he insisted on accompanying them.

He limped to the big throne-like boulder on the far side of the clearing and whistled to gather the rest of his men.

"Ravi, you're in charge. You know where the float's waiting for us." A farmer whose land spanned the lower foothills and a part of the plain had agreed to supply an anonymous float for the raiders. Gabrel didn't know, and didn't want to know, exactly how the farmer had scrounged a float that had no connection to him.

"Patrik, put on the other uniform; you'll sit up front with Ravi." Gabrel concealed a sigh. In all the planning for this trip, he had imagined himself beside Ravi, disguised in one of the enemy's self-fitting smartcloth uniforms, lying his way to the target. Oh, well. Patrik was the obvious replacement for him; best liar on the mountain. The danger was that he'd get carried away and say too much.

"Martin, Isak, stay out of sight in the back after you get the float loaded. I've paid Skyros for the use of their pack donkeys and their produce; they'll be loading up now and one of the boys will have them waiting for you behind the farm. They'll wait until you get back." He went on with the briefing, knowing he was emphasizing points he'd already made. But if he couldn't be with them, they had to know the plan by heart.

Eventually there was no more to say, and it was time for the four men to leave if they were to rendezvous with the Skyros pack train, shift the product into the float, and glide over the plains in time to reach their goal that night. Evening. They had to get there while their targets were still awake. Had he emphasized that enough?

* * *

The two young men in the uniform of the Harmony Expeditionary Force were not talking, and were running their transport float on low power. Apart from that, they did not seem to be making any particular effort to evade sentries.

"Be discreet, tactful, but not evasive," their chief had told them before they left. "They'll be much more suspicious if they spot you trying to sneak in. Remember – you may be, technically, breaking some of the Army's rules, but the one you're obviously breaking is one just about any sentry would wink at – particularly if you give him a sample."

"And if we run afoul of the one honest sentry in the camp?"

"Try to get past him somehow. Use your initiative." Gabrel's quick grin had flashed across his lean face. "Just bear in mind that leaving a trail of bodies is bound to get noticed. If you can stay inconspicuous this will be the perfect crime, because nobody will even know it happened Those idiots in B ring will just think they made a good trade with somebody on the outer perimeter."

That guidance was on Ravi's mind, but he still couldn't make himself steer the float right through the sentry line without first checking it out. He stilled the float behind a patch of bloodybush and raised his night-vision goggles to watch for the sentries. Gliding through the first perimeter would be easier, all round, than gambling that they had the right password and that the sentry who challenged them could be bribed with a sample of their cargo.

Finally, one soldier trudging the perimeter became visible as a green form at the edge of his vision. He walked slowly and deliberately along the trodden-down grass, continuously playing his blaster light around the outside of the perimeter. Ravi wished that his chosen bloodybush had more foliage, and prayed that no reflection would flash off his extremely undisguised float.

He stopped directly opposite their patch of bush and waited several seconds while the cold sweat trickled down Ravi's back. Had he somehow caught sight of them, a sense of their presence? If they were discovered hiding behind a bloodybush in a patch of Stinking Billy, it might be somewhat difficult to claim that this was just an innocent foraging party returning to base. Gabrel had *told* them...

Some people swore that they could sense when they were being stared at. Ravi didn't believe it, but just in case, he lowered his eyes to the float controls and depended on his sense of hearing.

After an eternity that lasted perhaps a minute and a half, the sentry sighed deeply, reversed course, and went back along the perimeter the same way as he'd come.

"One professional," Patrik murmured when the man was well on his way. "And maybe one lazy bum who is dozing instead of walking his sector?"

"He could just be late," Ravi responded. "Might show up any minute now."

Patrik could be counted on to make the most optimistic deduction possible in any set of circumstances. Ravi felt it his duty to balance things with an extra dose of pessimism. But as the minutes went by, he began to agree with Patrik's theory.

"If we wait long enough," Patrik prodded, "our professional sentry will come back on his next round."

True enough. The intelligence they'd gleaned from the locals was that each sentry had a relatively short stretch to guard. "All right, all right," Ravi muttered. "Let's go for it." He dropped the night-vision goggles so that he could steer past inanimate obstacles, backed the float away from the bloodybush and glided towards the point where the sentry had stopped and waited for his opposite number. Would coming into the camp from a place where two sentries met bolster their credibility? His shoulders tensed as they crossed the line, but the local intelligence was good again; there was no hidden barrier of sensors to catch them. The Army wasn't really worried about people crossing into the outer ring, and a sensor alarm would seriously inconvenience the locals who came as far as C ring daily with luxuries like fresh fruit to trade.

The outposts along C ring looked like little more than one-room syncrete squares printed with two windows and a door. The two nearest Ravi were lit up like a carnival, and from one of them came the rhythmic boom of Harmony's latest hit band. Good; those soldiers would be blinded *and* deafened by their own lights and music. And the ones in the two neighboring outposts wouldn't have much night vision left if they glanced at the Party Post. Ravi steered closer to the musical outpost. Getting past this bunch should be easy enough.

And it would have been, if one of the partying soldiers hadn't come outside to water a post. Or if Ravi had kept the goggles on. As it was, the float bumped against something soft and yielding. There was a thump and a curse. So much for the low profile.

"What the discord are you doing out here without lights?" the soldier grumbled, getting to his feet.

"Shhh!" Patrik said. "You don't want your friends to hear."

"I don't?" The man stood uncertainly, swaying a little on his feet. His breath stank of Harmony beer.

"Got something a little better than that sour beer here," Patrik murmured, laying a finger alongside his nose and winking. "What would you say to a jug of best lightning jack, straight from a mountain still?"

That sobered the soldier up in a hurry. "You serious? Lightning jack?"

"Have a taste if you don't believe me," Patrik said, uncorking the jug that he'd kept up front for just this purpose and offering it to the soldier.

The man put the top of the jug to his lips and tilted it back in preparation for a long, generous swallow.

A moment later he lowered the jug and breathed out harshly three or four times. "That's some powerful jack," he said though a suddenly raspy throat.

"You probably never had any before that wasn't watered down. Like I said, this is straight from the mountains."

"Discording right!" The soldier regarded the jug reverently.

"We got to deliver this load to our buyer, but we'll be happy to leave this jug with you in consideration of you not alerting any officers who just might disapprove."

"Who you delivering to?"

"Officers, of course. But you can be sure they'd disapprove of *you* having some. Be a terrible waste if they smashed all our jugs and poured the jack on the ground.

"Sure would," the soldier agreed. "Probably kill all the grass and stinkweed on the spot, too." He stared at the jug again, eyes narrowed. "This here's too much for one man, not enough to pass around. And if I don't drink it all, I got no place to hide it. Now *that* would be another turble waste, don't you agree?"

Patrik sighed elaborately. "I can see you're a sharp bargainer, friend. All right, it just about kills me to be giving this stuff away, but you can have *two* jugs. That should be enough to give you and the rest of the post a real happy night."

Ravi started breathing again after he had restarted the float and moved silently into the darkness between the rings of guard posts. "It worked."

"Of course. Gabrel said it would, didn't he?"

"Umm." Ravi was occasionally inclined to doubt their chief's omniscience. "These uniforms are good. It's like they were tailored to fit. Wish we could get smartcloth."

The uniforms would also add to their chances being shot as spies if they were caught. At least the two men hiding in the back of the float didn't have that risk. They'd probably just be shot on general principle.

"Yeah," Patrik agreed to distract himself from that overly pessimistic line of thought. "I don't suppose they contracted for smartcloth uniforms just to make life easier for anybody who wanted to steal a couple of them and pass as soldiers. One of those unforeseen consequences." He slowed the float to a near-standstill as the lighted huts of the B ring came into view. These posts were closer together than those in the C ring; a shout at one would be heard at the neighboring two. Oh, joy.

"It'll be the one on the right," Patrik said helpfully.

"*If* we came in at the exact same spot Peres described." There was no shortage of bloodybush patches outside the camp perimeter. Ravi handed the goggles to Patrik. "Use these and make sure we don't bump into another wandering soldier."

"And what will you be doing?"

"Driving. And looking for a way to identify B12." Ravi nudged the float forward at what felt like millimeters at a time. As they came closer to the squares of light shed by the guard posts, he gave a deep sigh of relief. "God bless the Army, they label everything. Got the number of each post on a tidy little sign. Here it is."

"I was right!"

"Almost," Ravi said drily. "Happens to be the one on the left, though."

The Ring B guard posts were larger than the C posts, probably printed from a two- or three- room program. Ravi navigated the float to just outside a door on the side of B12, then backed it off several feet. Just in case Peres had betrayed them, there was no point in parking right outside a door that could open on an array of fully powered blasters set to kill.

"What's that doing there?" Patrik suddenly asked.

There were two doors on this side but no windows, so they had to do without the faint light shed in front of the guard post. As Ravi's eyes recovered from the lighted area they'd just traversed, he saw what Patrik was referring to. A very tiny flitter, a single-person float, was settled discreetly in a dark corner where the post's back wall was augmented by a sort of shanty of irregular vines.

He shook his head. "Dunno. But I'm pretty sure it didn't carry a platoon of armed guards to intercept us. Probably it's something else these guys scrounged. Peres did say they're the most shameless thieves in the Army."

Still, the presence of the unexplained flitter added a little extra nervousness to Ravi's discreet scratch at the door.

* * *

Inside Outpost B12, the terminally bored soldiers had finished a meal consisting mainly of nanosludge and were lackadaisically fantasizing about what the officers quartered in Colony City were eating.

"Omelets," one suggested. "With real eggs, not that nanosynth crap."

"Pie," said Druett, who had a sweet tooth. "Thornberry pie, curd pie, chocolate pie…"

"Fellows, after we shift that thing," said Corporal Bollinjer, "we'll be able to trade for any kind of food we want." He jerked his head towards the closed door of the storage cabinet, which was apparently inadequate for their needs; most of the post's stores were neatly stacked in a corner of the main room.

"Yeah – once we shift it. Why couldn't you have nobbled something we could use instead of that?"

"Fellows, you just don't appreciate me. I am the unrecognized king of all the nobblers, wanglers, and scroungers in this man's army. When something that valuable 'falls off the back of the truck,' you don't pass on the opportunity just because it's not something you personally want. You take it and turn it into something you do want. Thanks to the general's views on abstinence, jugs of uncut lightning jack are as good as currency out here. B12 will be *famous* for its gourmet feasts. We can probably even invite *girls*."

"Girls…" the three sighed as one man, and their eyes were drawn to the door of the back room, which had been temporarily ceded to the fourth member of the group in view of his need for privacy.

"Kelso's probably the only happy grunt in B ring right now," Druett voiced their common thought.

"Yeah, but his girl will sneak back home in a couple of hours. And we'll still have the lightning jack."

"Shhh! Want her to hear? And tell?"

"She won't," the corporal said confidently. "Would Kelso get involved with a girl who'd split on us? Besides, there's no way she could tell anybody without also telling them where she'd been."

Heads nodded as the other two accepted their leader's reasoning. "All the same," said Druett, "it'd be cruel to interrupt Kelso now. We can make the trade without disturbing the lovebirds, and tell him about it after she's gone."

It was at that auspicious moment that Ravi scratched on the door.

* * *

If Ravi and Patrik had ever enjoyed the illusion that the trade had already been negotiated by Peres, Corporal Bollinjer of B12 destroyed it efficiently. "Not enough," he said bluntly after he stepped outside and played a beam of light over the contents of the float. "Only, what, twenty, twenty-five jugs. We agreed to trade for a full float-load of jack. You could have got a lot more in there. You trying to short us?"

"Oh, *stop*," Druett mourned under his breath at the corporal. "What if they go away again?"

"This is what we could get." Patrik felt it would be inadvisable to explain that the "extra" space had been taken up by two men

12

hiding in the back of the float. They were out now, presumably being very quiet and immobile until they were needed. But there'd been no time to rearrange the jugs to make them resemble anything close to a full load.

"Tell you what, you can have the printer for this but not the ink. To get the ink you'll have to bring us this much jack again."

"What if we can't get it?"

"Then you won't get the ink. And good luck printing air."

"Fair enough," Patrik conceded suddenly. If the plan he'd just thought of was to work, they needed to have nominally friendly relations with the four guys manning the post. "Damn natives cheated us too, they're bound to be holding more back. We'll just explain to them that cheating the cream of Harmony's army is a very, very bad idea." Ravi made a choking noise and Patrik stepped on his foot. "Meanwhile, want to give us a hand unloading this lot? Wouldn't do to break any jugs."

The three soldiers who'd greeted them were quite willing to carry jugs of lightning jack to the closet-sized "store room." Even with them helping Ravi and Patrik, it was a lengthy job. First the printer had to be removed; then they had to stack the jugs in the space around the cans of ink.

"Be a lot easier to store this if we just got the ink out of the way for you," Patrik mentioned casually.

The corporal's eyes narrowed. "Don't do us any favors. When you bring the second load, we'll let you take the ink."

"Where's your fourth man?" Ravi asked casually as he staggered inside with two jugs hanging from each hand. "Don't tell me the army's so hard up that they have to shortstaff the B ring too!" *Actually, do tell me that. It would be an excellent piece of news to bring back.*

13

To Ravi's disappointment, the guys of B12 chuckled and one of them jerked a thumb towards the closed door beside the storage closet. "Kelso's girl came visiting."

"We figured it would be cruel to interrupt them."

"Yeah, cruelty to dumb animals."

"And it's Kelso's problem if he's not out here for the first five… or six… or however many rounds."

When the last jugs were stacked, and the printer had been carefully conveyed to the float, Patrik sank down on the floor of the common room, leaning against a wall. "I'm bushed," he announced. "So's he," jerking his head at Ravi, who opened his mouth to deny it and then closed it again as he sat down beside Patrik.

"You guys on B ring must actually do all the calisthenics in the manual," Patrik said in admiring tones, "to be in such good shape." Actually he figured all three soldiers had aching muscles that would be painfully stiff by morning, but that wouldn't have been a friendly way to start the conversation that he wanted.

"Can't get out of it," Druett said, "not with an officer in every third outpost. You C-ring bastards have it easy."

"Guess so," Patrik agreed amiably. He locked his fingers together and stretched both arms forward, moaning slightly as he did so. "Whew! My back is *killing* me. How about a friendly drink, to set the seal on our new deal?

Bollinjer looked unhappy at the prospect of opening even one jug of the newly acquired treasure. *Greedy bastard.*

"Tell you what," said Ravi, "let's call this jug mine, and I'll bring you 26 jugs instead of 25 when I come back. Now how about a drink all round?"

Ravi opened the jug beside him and handed it to Bollinjer. "You guys go first. We can wait our turn."

All three soldiers reacted to the undiluted jack by coughing, gasping, and wiping suddenly watering eyes. None of them were paying enough attention to see how much Patrik and Ravi took.

"Another!" Ravi urged after pretending to take a deep swallow from the jug. "I see you're real men, with steady enough heads to take your liquor straight!"

That was good enough for another round, and also ensured that the men of Outpost B12 would have died before being seen to dilute the drink.

After those first two rounds, it became increasingly easy to find excuses for more. They drank to the C ring men who were the first line of defense, to the lazy privileged bastards sitting it out in A ring, and to the even lazier bastards living in the city, in real houses commandeered from the wealthier natives. Then they drank to Kelso's girl, to Kelso, and finally to Druett's dog back on Harmony.

The bottom of the jug was dangerously close when Corporal Bollinjer's head fell back and he began to snore.

"Can' holdsh liquor," Druett jeered. He tilted his head back to take one more swallow and just kept on leaning back and back until his head hit the syncrete wall and he slumped down beside Bollinjer.

"Don' worry 'bout Druett," O'Flangan reassured them, rescuing the jug. "Head'sh solid wo – woo- shtuff grows in the forest. Sholid trees. No, thash no' right."

"Have a drink to jog your memory," Ravi suggested.

O'Flangan looked surprised. "Ex'lent idea. Le's all have little drink. You too. They went off to sleep an' lef' me. You guys my boon c'mpanons now. All drink together." After that surprisingly lucid suggestion, he drained the jug and leaned back on Druett. "Nice sof' pillow. Haven't had pillow since I joined up. Druett'sh good guy." He rolled over on his back and began snoring.

"Actually," Ravi said as they began lugging the cans of printer ink out to the float, "that was impressive."

Patrik preened slightly. "Yes? And it was also impressive how quickly you picked up my idea and played along."

"Not you," Ravi said, "those guys. You realize it took almost a third of a jug of lightning jack each to put them out?"

"Let's just hope it keeps them out," Patrik said. Loading the ink was twice as hard as unloading the jugs, because the ink cans were small and extremely heavy and lacked handles. The job was further complicated by the fact that he and Ravi had to be careful not to step on any bits of drunken soldier sprawled out on the floor of the smallish room. They developed a sort of system: he and Ravi, the ones with uniforms, carried the ink cans to the door and handed them off to the other two for careful distribution around the float to balance the load.

* * *

"You don't have to go already, do you?" Kelso reached out from the floor, caressed Isovel's ankle and ran his hand up the back of her leg.

"I have to get my flitter back before the servants start work."

"Forget them. You don't need to worry about a bunch of native servants. They're all liars anyway."

"All Cretans are liars?" Isovel stood again and, hopping on one leg, drew on her trousers.

"Cretans? I thought they called themselves Esilians."

"Oh… Never mind." Isovel looked at Jonny Kelso's body in the shadowy room, remembered the sweet, gentle pressure of his lips, and reminded herself that there were more important things than being well read. It was unfair to be irritated with Jonny just because he hadn't had her opportunities.

"Stay a little longer?" Kelso returned to his main point.

"Do you *want* me to get caught?"

"At least then we wouldn't have to sneak around to be together."

"True," Isovel said. "We wouldn't be together at all, because Daddy would have me on the next ship back to Harmony! Don't you ever think beyond getting what you want in the moment?" The tunic was sticking to her hands and arms and crumpling at the back of her neck; with an irritated gesture she yanked at the back panel with both hands.

Naturally, nothing happened. You couldn't bully smartcloth; you had to persuade it. Isovel slid the tunic off again and stroked the back panel with both hands until it stretched, smoothed itself, and fell into a new shape loose enough to pull over her head and down over her slightly damp body. In a moment it would absorb the sweat on her skin and she would feel less irritable.

"You liked it well enough when I was concentrating on *you* in the moment," Jon said sulkily.

Isovel sighed. "Jonny, that's different –"

"'S what you always say. That and 'Never mind now.'" Jon said the last words in a high, squeaky voice that she supposed was an imitation of her own. "You think I'm too stupid to be worth talking to!"

"Don't be –" Isovel swallowed 'stupid' and substituted "annoyed, Jonny! If I thought you were stupid, would I take all these risks to be with you for a few hours?"

"Sure you would. That's how you get your kicks, innit? Slumming it with a grunt?"

Isovel slid her feet into her sandals. "That does it! I'm leaving now!" She'd had just about enough of that chip on Jonny's shoulder. She shoved the outer door open and stormed out into the night. With luck she could be in her flitter and headed back to the city before Jonny pulled his clothes on and came after her.

She walked straight into a patch of darkness that was, she belatedly recognized, just slightly denser and solider than the rest of the night. As she recoiled from the warm, solid chest she'd walked into, an arm around her waist kept her in place. Her captor spun her around effortlessly and put one hand over her mouth. "Patrik, don't come – "

He broke off as a young soldier stepped into the light from the open guardroom door, with something small but heavy in his hands. Not anyone she recognized from B12. And they seemed to have been loading up a heavy transport float. Stealing something from B12? Served the scroungers right – but where *were* the guys?

"Blast it!" said the young man called Patrik. "We were almost done. Ravi, we've got a problem here."

A second man in uniform came out. "I *know*. They're starting to wake up. We need to get going."

"*Another* problem," said Patrik, and at a nod of his head her captor stepped forward, pushing Isovel into the light.

"Kelso's girl?"

"What do we do with her, tie her up and gag her so she can't raise the alarm?"

"No time, and when they find her they'll know something happened. She'll just have to come along for the ride."

Isovel twisted desperately, bit, and got her mouth free for just a moment. "Jonny's right behind me. He'll kill all of you if you hurt me."

Her own scarf was crammed into her mouth and tied twice round her head.

The last thing she saw, just before she was thrown into the float, was Kelso running towards them.

He hadn't, after all, waited to get dressed.

CHAPTER TWO

The cave had a wide mouth that let in plenty of daylight for all practical purposes; all the same, Gabrel preferred to sit outside on sunny days. Like the solar cells that were brought out whenever it was dry enough, he felt that he was soaking up the sun's energy and recharging himself. This morning was so warm that he took off his shirt and set it on a nearby rock, folding it carefully. If only Esilia were allowed to produce its own smartcloth, clothing wouldn't be such a problem – warm layers for winter, waterproof ones for the rain that fell two days out of every three, dry socks – if he had a couple of yards of smartcloth, the first thing he'd do would be to make socks for everybody and then it wouldn't matter that they had to squelch through streams in their leaky boots.

Gabrel put his antique e-reader down on top of the shirt so that it too could recharge itself and limped back to the rock he had designated as a chair. He wished he could go down through the needle trees to meet his men. He should have been with them, dammit! But Jesse had threatened to hold him down and kick the other knee in if he wasted a good job of strapping by slithering down the mountain.

Chain of command wasn't an idea that had a strong following among the rebel groups.

His mouth twisted wryly. Some leader, lounging around and reading while other men took the risk! And now he wasn't even taking in the book he was supposed to be studying. He had wandered off into his own thoughts and hadn't actually read the last few paragraphs that his eyes had passed over.

Not that it really mattered. *Principles of Asymmetrical Warfare* didn't say anything about being a laundry master, a cook, a logistics clerk or any of the other roles that took up most of Gabrel's time. The section on logistics mostly dealt with carrying ammunition, which wasn't an issue with modern weapons. Food, the book said, would be supplied by loyal villagers.

The villagers were generous in sharing what they had – soft white cheese made from the milk of the native mountain doats, thin sour wine, the maize that was left after most of the crop went to the stills. But they couldn't be too much of a drain on any village's resources, and they had been in this location just an hour's climb from Skyros long enough that the villagers weren't exactly eager to give the guerrillas more than they had to. Which left Gabrel trying to figure out what he could use to make nanosludge taste like something. Well, at least Harmony had been generous with sludge; the first ship, so the story went, had arrived with five separate food-growing nanoswarms among a scant hundred deportees. Gabrel had to grant them that much. They hadn't meant to starve the people they exiled – just to separate them from all of civilization.

In the generations since then, the deportees had learned how to irrigate the forbidding red plains that made up ninety percent of the continent, to grow their own food and to herd the native harbeests and doats for meat. As well, they'd developed a system to integrate the new deportees who came on each ship, endlessly, until you would have thought the entire population of Harmony was being exiled as political criminals.

Nearly a quarter of the first deportees had been of Greek origin, and a hundred years of life on this planet had not erased their cultural memories. Where sane people looked at the mountains and saw harsh rocks, not enough soil, and an endless battle to catch the snow melt that came down from the freezing peaks, Greeks saw home and freedom. They disappeared into the hills where Harmony's authority barely reached, built stone houses clinging to the mountainsides and thrived. But life was still hard in the mountains by plains farmers' standards. There was little space for crops, they depended on the scrawny mountain doats for meat and milk, and the lack of transportation held the whole district back.

The long morning shadows were shortening. Why weren't his men back yet? Had they failed? Been captured? How long could it take to drag a train of donkeys up the mountain?

Gabrel looked around the small grassy patch in front of the cave, with its guardian ring of close-packed needle trees. The trees baking in the sun released their sharp, resinous scent, intoxicating in the mountain air. It was a good location; on two sides the plateau broke away in steep cliffs, while behind the cave the mountain went up almost as steeply, with patches of pebbly scree that would rain down warning pebbles on them if anybody tried to approach from above.

Nikos would be perched on a ledge up there, ready to give a warning whistle if anybody they didn't know was spotted coming this way – though the danger of being found was slight. The only way to reach this dell was via the labyrinth of winding, narrow trails through the needle woods, and in their first days here Ravi and Nikos had made a point of trampling and enlarging trails that led only into thornberry thickets, while training vines over the almost invisible paths that led to the cave. Gabrel hoped that Ravi remembered how to get from Skyros to here. Maybe he should have sent Nikos so that he could act as a guide for the last leg of the journey. But Nikos was only seventeen… The path would, of course, be much more obvious after he and Patrik brought the pack donkeys along it; well, no help for that. They'd just have to try to obscure it again afterwards.

The other men had casually wandered off after breakfast, one to hunt for anything that would improve the non-flavor of plain sludge, the other two most likely to visit one of the home-made distilleries that clung to the mountainside in secluded places. The governors of Esilia had long felt that lightning jack, the mountain region's most valuable product, should be taxed; the mountain people, naturally, disagreed. They were unfriendly enough to plainsmen to discourage all but the most enthusiastic tax gatherers, and for double security, they set up their distilleries in places that you'd think even a mountain doat would have trouble reaching.

Plainsmen like Patrik said that of course the villagers had a natural advantage, being half mountain doat themselves. They had a number of jokes about cloven hooves, hairy tails, and branching antlers.

Give the boy credit: he'd learned quickly not to make those jokes where the mountain villagers could hear him – and more than half the men in Gabrel's band were mountaineers. It only took one black eye and a couple of bruised ribs for him to get the message.

A piercing whistle from high on the mountainside broke Gabrel's reverie. He scanned the close-packed needle trees for any sign of movement. The dark green needles were shaking over to the left… and there, and there…

Amari and Jesse on the right, and Wil on the left, broke through the screen of needles almost simultaneously. Nikos could be heard incautiously scrambling down to them across the patches of scree, and incidentally sending down a shower of pebbles and raw shards of rock that inspired all of them to duck under the cover of the cave's wide mouth.

"They're back!" Nikos announced before he was quite level with the rest of them. He made a flying leap from the ledge over the cave to the patch of grass below, and landed so lightly that Gabrel envied him. When he'd been seventeen, he would have made the jump too. Dammit, twenty-three wasn't exactly old; he could leap all over the mountainside just like Nikos if he wanted to, he told himself. It was the responsibility of command, the understanding of how even a minor injury could fatally slow a man, that forced him to take the safer paths.

And, of course, his own – not quite so minor – injury, incurred on last week's raid. Gabrel's knee twinged in protest as he stood to greet the returning men.

Besides, Nikos had grown up in one of the mountain villages that clung to the sides of these hills, so he had a built-in advantage.

"How many?" Amari demanded, and simultaneously Wil asked, "Did they get it?"

Nikos looked first at Amari, opened his mouth to speak, caught Gabrel's eye, swallowed, and stood at attention looking only at Gabrel. "Sir! I have to report a large party advancing. Leaders are identified as Ravi and Patrik, and… somebody I don't know. Riding a donkey. The guy I don't know, I mean. And they're bringing a train of a dozen pack donkeys. Heavily loaded."

"They got it! Hai yi!" Amari shouted.

'Hai yi yi yiee!" Nikos joined in, sending the call to bounce off the mountainside and echo on the far side of the valley.

"Don't let's advertise our presence to everybody in the valley," Gabrel suggested mildly.

"Aw…. They already know we're here. We get eggs and cheese from Skyros 'most every day," Nikos argued.

Gabrel quelled him with a look. "Consider it practice for the day when a Harmony patrol shows up in Skyros." He turned back to the others. "All right, they're going to be tired. Make a chain to unload and place the supplies back in the cave."

"I'd just killed," Wil objected. "A nice plump wild doat. She'll be dragged off by scavengers before we finish unloading."

"Are you *absolutely sure* she hasn't already been dragged off, and you stuck with spending an hour looking for her with no result?" Wil did seem to have urgent tasks elsewhere quite predictably when there was heavy labor to be done. He hadn't been there when it was time to dig a latrine, or when they built the wall of woven needle tree branches for extra cover.

Wil held up his hands, palms outward to show the blood. "I swear on my mother's grave, this time I'm telling the truth."

That would have been slightly more impressive if Gabrel hadn't known that Wil's mother was alive and energetically managing the family farm down on the plains. "Very well. You can go, but if you don't come back with a field-dressed doat, don't bother to come back at all, understand?"

"Stupid," Amari murmured as Wil disappeared behind the green wall of needles, "and lazy. Who'd miss the triumphant return just to avoid carrying a few packs of supplies to the cave?"

The needles quivered violently again and Patrik pushed into the clearing. Gabrel let out his breath in silent relief. He'd sent four men, nearly half his group, on this mission. He hoped to get back four men in reasonably good shape. But Patrik, just two years older than Nikos and not noticeably more mature, had been the one he worried about most.

"Everybody all right?" he demanded sharply.

Patrik was breathing heavily. "Better than all right," he announced with a seraphic smile before taking another gasp of air. "Got what we came for, and a bonus!"

"What's that?"

Patrik slowly folded his lanky frame down upon the grass where he'd been standing. "Only two things wrong with the mountains," he announced. "You people don't keep enough oxygen around, and there is *way* too much vertical."

"So hang onto a donkey's tail, next time, instead of rushing ahead to be first back," Gabrel said crisply. "The bonus?" Dear God, had Patrik gotten creative again? He'd been counting on Ravi to restrain him.

"It'll be here in a minute." Patrik pulled off the top half of his uniform and used it to mop his forehead. "*I* think it should be a surprise, and Ravi thinks it should wait until he has a chance to explain."

Gabrel's forebodings grew. It sounded as though Ravi hadn't been quite as successful as he'd hoped at keeping Patrik within bounds. But he could hear the donkey train now, crashing through the woods and, no doubt, turning the narrow path to their camp into something more like a construction road. No need for a show of authority; he'd know the worst within minutes anyway.

The first donkeys came through the trees, with Ravi tugging on their headstalls while the donkeys looked this way and that and indicated that they'd just as soon wander off into the woods if only this stupid person weren't being so insistent. One of the first pair of donkeys was loaded with nets on either side, each holding two cans that looked very much like the ink they'd gone to get. The other – was being ridden by what Gabrel supposed was Patrik's 'surprise.'

"Pat! You've never gone and brought me a girl for my birthday?" Amari was the first of them to overcome his shock and find his voice.

"You have succeeded," Gabrel told Patrik. "That is definitely a surprise. Ravi, I'm told you can explain?"

Before Ravi could speak, the girl slipped off the donkey and addressed Gabrel directly. "Are you in command of this rabble?" The cut-glass, icy voice seemed incongruous, coming from a sweat-stained and dusty girl with a mop of pale hair falling around her face. Her long dark green trousers and lighter green tunic appeared spotless and unwrinkled and generally in much better shape than the girl. Smartcloth, then. And that accent had never come from Esilia.

"One moment, Citizen." The girl's expression told Gabrel that he'd guessed correctly. He turned on the men, who were all staring at the girl like idiots, and probably frightening her. "Ravi, what part of 'inconspicuous' did you not understand? And the rest of you 'rabble', don't just stand there. We've got a pack train to deal with. All of you get to work! Unload the donkeys, put the ink in the cave, and the printer – you did get the printer?"

Ravi nodded. "Martin and Isak are preventing it from falling out of a sling between the last two donkeys. Hell of a thing to wrestle up a mountain."

"Printer at the front of the cave, when it gets here. Take the donkeys to water as they're unloaded, then get them back down the mountain as far as Skyros; we paid enough to use them, we're not going to feed them as well. Do I have to spell out everything for you?"

"Water?" the girl repeated, then closed her mouth with a snap. Obviously she'd be damned if she asked them for anything.

"Allow me." Nikos had kept his wits; while everybody else was staring, he'd taken his flask to the spring and filled it. Now he handed it to the girl, who took the flask in her bound hands, sipped cautiously and then tilted her head back to inhale the entire contents of the flask. "Skyros water is known to be the best in all the mountains," Nikos boasted, "and Skyros gets its water from our spring."

"Skyros is also known for its talkative men," Gabrel said drily. "Nikos, get to work. Ravi, you're excused from unloading duty while you give me an explanation."

Ravi and Patrik alternately described the scene outside B12 as they had just finished loading the cans of ink: the girl appearing out of nowhere, the hasty decision to throw her in the float and take off, the naked man pursuing them. "Once she'd seen us," Patrik pointed out, "'inconspicuous' was really no longer an option. Whether we took her or left her, somebody was bound to notice."

"Ask them what they did to Jonny," the girl interrupted. "They wouldn't tell me anything."

"Jonny would be the – ah – scantily dressed gentleman?" Gabrel inquired. He cocked an eyebrow at Ravi.

Ravi shrugged. "We didn't even bring any lethal weapons. All we had was two stunners. Martin and Isak both aimed at him. He hit the ground hard. He should be all right now, except for stunner hangover."

"And his buddies," Patrik said with a smirk, "are probably having a multi-colored lightning jack hangover."

"All right. That explains why you took off with her," Gabrel said, "you were stupid, and you panicked." Ravi's brown cheeks flushed, but Patrik clamped his jaw with an expression remarkably like a donkey's. "But you had forty kilometers of plains to cross before you had to hide the float and load the pack train. Why didn't you stop somewhere, put her off and let her walk back? Leave her far enough from any farms, she wouldn't have been able to raise the alarm in time."

"Well, Patrik thought…" Ravi began.

"Was Patrik in charge of this expedition? I thought I put *you* in charge."

"He had a point…"

"I recognized her," Patrik said proudly. "She's General Dayvson's daughter."

The girl laughed. Loudly. "Oh, you idiots. Do I look like a general's daughter?"

Even after a forced ride through the mountains, Gabrel thought, she looked exactly like a general's daughter – or the daughter of somebody else from the top rung of Committee families. It wasn't so much the long, slim legs, clad in perfectly fitted smartcloth; or the once-white hands, now marred with several scratches and a broken nail; or even the patrician profile. It was the way she lifted her chin and talked down her elegant nose at them, he thought. And she did resemble the girl he'd seen on holocasts, except for being considerably more disheveled.

"I've seen the newscasts," Patrik insisted. "They showed you debarking with your father, off a troopship from Harmony."

"That was nearly two months ago. Don't you keep up with the news?"

"We can't get the 'casts in the mountains. Only when we go down to the plains."

"Well. I suppose that explains it. You yokels obviously haven't heard. Isovel Dayvson went back to Harmony after a week."

Among the men unloading the donkeys, Jesse paused with a can of ink in his hands, put it down and drifted closer to the group. Gabrel noted the movement out of the corner of his eye. He'd deal with Jesse later. In this case he couldn't simply shout and trust his authority to get obedience. They needed Jesse for his medical training, but it was a hard bargain. Jesse was the kind of built-in discipline problem that could wreck a group; ten years older than Gabrel and so bitter about Harmony's treatment of his family that he was a simmering mass of barely-contained violence.

Patrik scowled. "And you just happen to be her identical twin separated at birth, I suppose?"

"You. Captured. The. Wrong. Woman," the girl insisted. "I'm just a commissary clerk. Don't tell me you really believed those stories about Dayvson keeping his own daughter in an occupied city! Haven't you Esilian hicks ever heard of propaganda?"

"Well, you see," Gabrel said apologetically, "It's not just that idiot Patrik. All of us hicks get to see some of them flashy holos when we go down-country. And you do look a lot like Isovel Dayvson to me."

"And me," Ravi chimed in.

The girl shrugged. "I daresay all civilized women look alike to you bumpkins. No wonder this is the poorest sector of the colony. Look at you men lolling around here half-naked instead of doing some useful work!"

Patrik flushed and pulled his shirt back over his head. Scowling at Patrik, Gabrel stuck his thumbs in the waistband of his pants and pushed them down another inch, until they were hanging off his hipbones. They weren't going to take lessons in etiquette from some Harmonica snob of a girl, and the sooner she grasped that, the better.

Her fair skin showed a flush more clearly than did Patrik's olive complexion. She blinked and stared Gabrel directly in the eyes.

Her own eyes were a light golden brown, about two shades darker than her tumbled hair. Of course, there was no reason to suppose any of that was natural. Gabrel didn't know what kind of mods a top-level Harmony cosmetic stylist was offering these days, but hair and eye color coordination was probably the least of it.

"I suppose you think you'll get a fortune in ransom for me? Well, don't blame me when General Dayvson laughs in your faces."

"If she's the wrong one," growled Jesse, "why shouldn't we kill her now and save the trouble of keeping her?" He stepped forward so swiftly that he had her by the shoulder, his knife bright against her throat, before anyone else could react.

"Oh, she's Dayvson's daughter, all right," said Gabrel tiredly. "She just doesn't know when to give up. Just like her father. Stand down, Jesse. Or – if you feel an uncontrollable urge to use that knife – you might cut her hands free."

She yanked her bound hands back when Jesse touched her wrist. "Don't be afraid," he said. "Yet."

"I'm not afraid, I just don't want you destroying the only sash I've got! Can't somebody just untie it?" She extended her hands to Gabrel, who looked at Patrik's work with dismay. Patrik had wound the soft, voluminous silky fabric several times around the girl's wrists and had finished with hard, tight knots that sank into the fabric.

With a conscious effort, he did not limp for the three steps that brought him close enough to work on the sash. His knee flamed white-hot agony on the second step, but he could live with that; better than appearing a cripple before this rude, scornful young woman.

He had to stand quite close to her to pick at the knots; close enough to notice that although she smelled primarily of sweaty human female, there was also a hint of a gentle floral fragrance about her. Wisps of her loosened fair hair brushed his face.

His hands were *not* shaking, it was just difficult loosening the knots. He bent his head over them and concentrated on the sash, not on the fine white hands and delicate wrists it bound. Patrik had made this mess, it would serve him right to have to fix it. But Patrik was young, not so steady, and he might be influenced by the scent, the closeness. He, being more mature, could take it in stride... She was tall for a woman, just his height, presumably staring out over his bent head while he worked... There went the last knot.

Freed, she shook out her wrists for a moment, then lifted her hands and tried to run her fingers through the long hair that rippled in the sunlight where it wasn't hopelessly tangled. "I don't suppose anyone has a comb? No? Why am I not surprised?"

"Us bumpkins don't comb our hair much," Patrik said.

"And neither, it seems, will I. Until you come to your senses and send me back. Kidnapping me was a very big mistake, you know."

Gabrel was more than half inclined to agree with her on that point.

"Send who back?" Patrik challenged her. "Isovel Dayvson – or the conveniently anonymous clerk?"

The girl caught her hair up in both hands, twisted it at the back of her head, and quickly wrapped it into a loose bun, with a final

33

twist that tucked the loose ends under the rest of the tangled, cloudy mass. "You can call me Tiffni."

"You don't look anything like a Tiffni!"

She sighed. "All right. If you want me to be Isovel Dayvson, then I'm Isovel Dayvson. Happy now?"

CHAPTER THREE

General Dayvson's first act on disembarking on the rebel continent had been to commandeer the governor's mansion as general headquarters for the army and living space for himself, his aides, and Isovel. Governor Serman was not happy about being booted down to the next-best house in Colony City, whose space and amenities were far below those of the mansion. Since Dayvson regarded Wilyam Serman as a fool whose cruelty had directly inspired the present rebellion, and himself as the sensible man who'd been sent to retrieve the situation, he was impervious to Serman's grouching. The governor's mansion was the only building in Colony City that could house him and his immediate staff and still provide rooms for meetings and staff work. The governor's creature comforts were not his concern.

Jaymi Kamron, Dayvson's secretary, was not an imaginative man. On most days he enjoyed his job, which he understood to consist of filtering all the demands for the general's attention and directing them to the appropriate staff member while bringing only the potentially immediate disasters to Dayvson's desk. "It's the perfect job," he would say to young line officers who twitted him about never getting actual combat experience. "All of the power of command and none of the responsibility. *I* wouldn't want to deal with the baskets of unexploded bombs I pass on to the general, but then I don't have to; I just need to recognize them when they come in."

Up until yesterday, that had never been a problem.

Now something with the potential to explode right in his face had come across his desk. The obvious thing to do was to pass it to the general immediately, before it stopped ticking. But that would involve confessing that he'd mistaken a bomb for a minor clusterfark yesterday, and the general just might explode in his face over that.

Chord and Consonance knew, the atmosphere in HQ had been explosive enough since the general discovered yesterday that his daughter had left the mansion the previous night and had never returned. Corporals were reporting to sergeants, sergeants were standing at attention and reporting to lieutenants, lieutenants were tearing out their hair and having every house in Colony City searched.

In the midst of all that, Kamron had not thought the report from B ring about a single outpost's bizarre breach of discipline worth bothering any of the general staff. The corporal and the three privates posted to B12 had apparently been reported to B-Sergeant Krayg for drunk and disorderly behavior, indecent exposure, and possession of a truly amazing number of jugs of prohibited liquor. Krayg wanted Corporal Bollinjer busted down to private and transferred to C ring, the three privates transferred to C ring with an emphasis on latrine duties, and four steady men sent out to replace the delinquent foursome. All that required no more than drafting a series of routine staffing directives which Kamron was fully empowered to sign on his own authority.

Krayg had assured him that all the prohibited liquor had been destroyed. Kamron was privately skeptical about that, but he felt quite sure that any party sent out from HQ would find nothing but some broken jugs. He told Krayg that he had better be quite sure the lightning jack had been destroyed, because any further reports of drunken parties in B ring would result in his demotion. That was probably enough of a warning to make Krayg cautious about letting any of B ring get hold of enough of the stuff to become more than cheerful and slightly cross-eyed. As long as there were no more drunken orgies, Kamron was willing to turn a blind eye to the quantities of lightning jack on the ring. The possibility of getting a drink from the sergeant should, if anything, improve response time and accuracy from the outposts in B ring. Hard liquor might not be officially permitted in Harmony's army, but the prospect of an unofficial drink or three from time to time was an excellent motivator for bored soldiers.

There had seemed, then, no reason to bother the general with a story of soldiers misbehaving as all soldiers would, given the chance.

Now there were two papers on Jaymi Kamron's desk that could, if mixed, prove dangerously combustible.

One was a note from Sergeant Krayg asking what should be done with the single-seater flitter found at post B12, which all four soldiers denied knowing anything about.

The other was... or purported to be... a message from the Free Esilian Army, saying that they had Isovel Dayvson and promising that no harm would come to her as long as there were no more reprisals carried out on the innocent farmers and craftsmen of Esilia.

Dayvson was pacing his office – formerly the Governor's Small Dining Room – when Jaymi knocked at the door.

"Any news?" he demanded, and in almost the same breath, "Sit. I've thought of some new search orders."

"I… uh… thought you should read this first." Kamron handed him the crudely hand-printed flimsy purporting to be from the Free Esilians.

Dayvson did not shout, curse, or throw small pieces of office furniture as he read the flyer. He did, however, emit a small hissing noise that made Kamron look for a sheltered place to dive in case the furniture-throwing started.

"It's a threat," he stated.

"Yes, sir."

"A damned impudent threat!"

"Yes, sir."

"And stupid beyond belief! Don't they understand that the random reprisals were that idiot Serman's idea, and that I'm here to – among other things – stop them?"

"It seems they may not be entirely clear on that point, sir."

"Well, we can't let them get away with this."

"Ah… no, of course not, sir."

"I'll say one thing for that sadistic idiot Serman, the City and the plains villages are quiet now. Not the way I would have chosen, but not unknown in the history of warfare."

"Sir?"

Dayvson tapped his reader. "I was just reading about a similar policy this morning. 'They make a desert, and call it peace.' An ancient historian on his people's habits. He also says… Well, never mind. Why are you distracting me with these nonessentials?" He tapped again to shut down the translation of Tacitus and glared at Kamron. "These louts kidnapped my daughter! We have to send out an expeditionary force immediately to teach them a lesson."

"And rescue your daughter?" Kamron added after waiting a moment in case the general wanted to say anything more.

"Hm? Oh, yes, yes, and retrieve Isovel. What was she thinking anyway, to get herself kidnapped by the damned rebels? How could it have happened?"

"She might have been… um… closer to the outer ring than was advisable. Her flitter was found at an outpost in B ring."

"Which outpost? Have the soldiers been questioned?"

"Yesterday it was not possible to question them thoroughly. They all had blinding hangovers – though one man claims he didn't drink anything, he was caught by a stunner beam. And Sergeant Krayg said that he did seem somewhat more… neurologically impaired… than the other three." What Krayg had actually said was more along the lines of "about as sharp as a bowl of sludge *before* they started drinking."

"Discord! You knew about this yesterday? Why wasn't I told?"

"I didn't know about the flitter yesterday, sir. That wasn't in the reports. At that time it looked like a simple case of disorderly conduct, nothing worth bothering you with." Kamron proffered the two flimsies relating to the B12 incident, the one from yesterday and the inquiry about the flitter from today.

Dayvson scowled over the flimsies. "Did anybody think to ask how these grunts got hold of a roomful of lightning jack jugs in the first place?"

"I don't know," Kamron admitted. "Sergeant Krayg didn't say anything about that."

"Sloppy work. Damned sloppy. I want all four of these men here within an hour. Well? What are you waiting for?"

"On it, sir!" Kamron took this as permission to escape.

Left alone in his office, General Dayvson picked up his reader again. Tacitus' reflections on the decline of political freedom in the Roman Empire had given him some insights into the history of

Harmony, but that wasn't what he needed now. He needed some account of an expeditionary force into hostile territory, preferably with details – lots of details – about organization and logistics.

That was the trouble with making this up as he went along. As the only sovereign nation on this world, Harmony had never fought a war, never anticipated having to fight one, and did not maintain a standing army. The revolt in the colony took them by surprise, and the Committee had attempted to create an army on the spur of the moment. Or rather, they had tasked Dayvson, the closest thing Harmony had to a military historian, with doing so.

He'd only had time for a quick overview of ancient military organization and ranks, and the main thing he got from that was that an army ran on the competence of its NCO's. So Harmony's peace officers became sergeants and corporals in the new army, and the ranks were filled with draftees. He sometimes shuddered at the necessity of allowing the soldiers in the outer defense rings fully charged weapons on the basis of three days' training, but what could he do? They couldn't be expected to defend the capital against a rebel attack by throwing rocks, could they? But ever since he'd set up the rings, he'd been expecting some disaster.

He just hadn't expected *Isovel* to get herself embroiled in it.

Dayvson tried to put the girl out of his mind and concentrate on his reading. Either she was all right or she wasn't, and in any case he expected to learn that she had got herself kidnapped by taking some idiotic risk and it was all her own fault. And knowing Isovel, he expected that her kidnappers were almost certainly regretting their action by now.

Which was neither a comforting reflection, nor a help in concentrating on his new reading matter: a translation of Caesar's

Gallic Wars describing his multiple invasions and campaigns in the barbarian lands beyond the Roman empire. As a history professor Dayvson had cited the clarity of the writing and had invited students to consider the political consequences of Caesar's campaigns. Now he was looking for a much lower level of detail. How were the legionaries armed? What was the order of march? How did they protect the marching column from sudden attacks by hostile natives?

"And I strongly suspect," he murmured, "that my opposite number in the Esilian Free Army is reading Mao and Guevara on how to conduct guerrilla warfare."

Until Kamron brought the grunts to his office, Dayvson dictated notes on whatever he found in Caesar's book into his wristcom, more as a way of forcing himself to concentrate than because he was getting a lot of useful technical information.

One look at the four miscreants who had formerly staffed B12 clarified a great deal for the general.

"Private Kelso. I begin to understand... much." Kelso, being even more lacking in military skills than the average draftee, had begun his army career as an orderly working for the staff in the governor's mansion. Dayvson had sent the man to relieve some other private in an outer-ring guard post when he began to suspect that an unsuitable friendship was growing between Kelso and his daughter. He never had understood that: Kelso was nowhere near up to Isovel's weight, culturally or intellectually, and he would have thought the private would have bored her silly within a few weeks.

And so he might have, Dayvson thought ruefully, if he himself had had the good sense to ignore the incipient affair. By transferring Kelso, he had given the young man the glamor of the forbidden. Isovel doubtless had a holo to keep her reminded of his striking good looks, and now he was not present daily to remind her of his stupidity.

"Night before last. While you four were singing, dancing, and showing the neighboring outposts all you'd got. Dare I hope that my daughter had left before you began your swinish display?"

"Haven't seen Citizen Miss Dayvson since I left service here, sir," Kelso lied gallantly.

"Stop trying to protect her reputation!" Dayvson snapped. "The issue now is *saving her life.* I want to know everything about your movements – and hers – on that evening."

Within short order he got most of that information: the acquisition of a large supply of lightning jack from "a couple of guys from C ring,"; the sequence of toasts that had left the other two privates and the corporal somnolent on the floor; Kelso and Isovel in the back room, somehow not noticing all this activity; the spat which had sent Isovel stamping out the side door and into the arms of the C ring guys; their tossing her into the float and taking off while Kelso gave a futile chase that was ended when his head crossed paths with a stunner beam.

"Be glad it was only a stunner," Dayvson told him. "*I* would have used a blaster. I still might." He looked wistful. It would probably be wrong to kill Kelso personally; he'd have to look at that other book, the Uniform Code of Military Justice, to see just what the leader of an army was permitted to do to traitors. Because he was quite sure that, knowingly or not, these four had conspired to commit treason.

"You haven't told me everything. *No,*" he snapped as Kelso began a stammering, roundabout reply, "I do not want to know why you were naked at the time. I *do* want to know why you did not immediately report my daughter's abduction."

"Sir," said Kelso with an air of conscious virtue, "due to my attempts to rescue Isovel, I was stunned and remained unconscious for thirty, no, thirty-two hours after the incident."

"And you three?" Dayvson whirled on the drunks, who still looked rather pale and greenish even thirty-eight hours after their jack party.

"When we came to," Corporal Bollinjer explained, "we didn't know anyone had been abducted. Kelso was unconscious, his girl wasn't there, and our – some of our stuff had been stolen by those bastards from C."

Bollinjer remained adamant that none of them had known the identity of Kelso's girl friend, but under Dayvson's sharp questioning the rest of the story came out – most of it, anyway. The men at B12 had somehow got hold of a 3-D small-arms printer and a generous supply of the steel particles in colloidal solution that constituted its "ink." Since they already had their issue blasters, they had been looking to trade the printer for something they could actually use. When the native orderly who looked after B10, B11 and B12 told them he knew some guys on C who wanted more small arms, it had seemed like a reasonable story to them; the C ring guard posts were out there on the edge of civilization and in the event of a rebel mob attack, they might well want to have a good supply of blasters charged and ready. The offer of a float load of pure mountain lightning jack in trade had short-circuited any critical thinking they might have applied to the story.

"It did not occur to you," Dayvson inquired awfully, "to ask how a couple of privates on C ring acquired enough lightning jack to make all of B12 drunk and leave more to use as trade goods?"

Corporal Bollinjer shuffled his feet and studied the toe caps of his boots. "Sir, it's sort of an accepted rule out there. You don' ask how anybody else acquired stuff to trade, and they don' ask about your stuff."

"And since Kelso woke up and told you that they'd taken my daughter as well as your – er – trade goods, it did not occur to you that she could have *walked* back from C ring by now? Or returned to B12 to get her flitter?"

"Sir," the corporal said desperately, "we din't know she was your daughter. We din't know she was missing. We been in trouble ever since we come to, and din't nobody *tell* us anything. They sure axed a lot of questions, though."

"I put it to you," General Dayvson said, "that the people who 'bought' your printer and ink were not from C ring at all. They brought that lightning jack all the way from the mountains. They were, in fact, members of the Esilian Free Army – and I can have you all up on charges of treason for selling munitions to the enemy!"

"They was wearing regular army uniforms!" O'Flangan protested.

"You can't *know* they was rebels!"

"Din't anybody search C ring for the printer and ink… and… your daughter?"

Kelso was the only silent one. Perhaps he was brighter than Dayvson had estimated.

Marginally.

"What about the native who brokered the trade?"

He wasn't really surprised to hear that the man had failed to show up for work and that his address had turned out to be a deserted patch of red rocks.

Dayvson shoved the flyer from the Esilian Free Army at them. There was a certain amount of mumbling and sounding out words – Harmony really had given him the scum of the country to build into an army – but as the meaning sank in, they paled and sagged slightly – all but Kelso, who took two strides to the desk, leaned over to get closer to the general, and shouted, "Why are *you* wasting time? We have to rescue her before – before those savages –"

"*I*," General Dayvson said icily, "will lead a column into the mountains to rescue my daughter. *You*, having demonstrated your criminal incompetence and stupidity, will be here – in the stockade – where you may think over your defenses."

"We have a stockade?"

"We will by tomorrow." Dayvson made a mental note to tell Kamron to detail men and supplies for an instant stockade. A small one should do. "Until then we will keep you in the basement."

"Defenses? Plural?" That was Kelso again.

"You will be brought up on charges upon my return, make no mistake about that. If Isovel cannot be rescued, you will most certainly be charged with treason and found guilty. I believe that is a death penalty offense." And if the Universal Code of Military Justice disagreed, it would just have to be edited.

"If Isovel returns unharmed... "He paused for a long moment, "the charges may – *may* be slightly reduced. I strongly recommend that you spend your time in the basement tonight searching your memories. Any detail that you can recall might be useful to us."

CHAPTER FOUR

—➤ ◄—

A light drizzle was enough to make the mountainside cold and damp. It had inspired most of Gabrel's group to sleep inside the cave the previous night, but apparently it wasn't enough to stop them setting off on their project – whatever it was – that day. Isovel had been unhappy about sharing sleeping space with what she privately called "the rabble of rebels," but now she admitted to herself that it hadn't been all bad. The guerrillas had mostly stopped staring at her, they'd been generous with their offers of blankets to soften the cave floor and to keep her warm, and the temperature-balancing smartcloth together with their combined body heat had made the cave almost comfortable. Apart from the crowding, she'd gone on camping trips with her crêche-mates that had been worse.

And Gabrel had assigned her a niche at the base of the cave wall, and had slept with his body interposed between her and the rest of the rebel rabble.

Not that that had made any difference, or mattered in the slightest. They were all rebels, terrorists, probably murderers and rapists to judge by the newsers' broadcasts, and there was no reason to trust this

Gabrel any more than the rest of the rabble. Maybe less, considering the way he'd been swaggering around without his shirt yesterday.

So, logically speaking, she should have been terrified to be left alone with him today. Isovel tried to encourage the fear any decent woman of Harmony would feel in such circumstances, and found only a deep, traitorous sense of contentment. If you were under shelter, it could be soothing to watch the light rain falling just outside. The presence of the terrorist leader reassured her that she hadn't been abandoned. And there was something almost – pleasant – in the warmth of two people sitting together, sharing body heat under one blanket.

"So where have the rest of your crew gone, and why aren't you with them?" Isovel asked idly.

"Twisted my knee last week. And they're not all gone," Gabrel told her, "they're just not in here. I've got one man at the regular guard post, one watching from the trees, and one waiting to receive and relay messages. And one watching the captive – that would be me."

"You don't need to do that," Isovel said. "I couldn't even begin to retrace the path we took to get here – especially the part we traversed in the dark."

"Oh, I know that," Gabrel said. "I'm just not entirely sure you know it."

"I lived my whole life in Harmony City. I'm lost without a map and street signs." She hoped that sounded convincing. How hard could it be to get to the plains? All she'd have to do was go downhill.

"So you are," Gabrel agreed, "but it would be much simpler for everybody if you actually believed it. For now, though, just in case you're thinking you could get away from a man with a bum knee, you might want to consider the sentries I've set out."

"How do you know they're not just taking a nap under the nearest shelter?"

Gabrel grinned. The momentary smile made him look much younger, almost boyish. Then the usual tension returned to his face, and he looked what Isovel knew him to be – the ruthless commander of a band of terrorists. "Do your soldiers nap when they're on sentry duty?"

"I suspect some of them do," Isovel confessed. "And you already know that they'll get drunk, given the chance. The officers aren't sure what to do about it. None of them have much training."

"I'm not surprised. Seems to me that the problem for your people is that you don't know how to organize an army."

"And you do?" she snapped.

"Well, it's a bit different. We don't have an army to organize. That saves us a lot of the problems you Harmonicas are having."

"My father," Isovel said icily, "is Harmony's foremost military historian. If anybody can organize an army, he should be able to do it." She had given up the pretense that she wasn't General Dayvson's daughter.

"Mmm. Military history tends to be long on theory and short on detail. I should know, I've been reading the books Colonel Travis recommended."

"*Studying?*" It wasn't how Isovel pictured terrorists spending their spare time.

Gabrel shrugged off the blanket and stretched his arms out in front of him, hands back to back and fingers interlocked. The action generated a ripple of muscle under his shirt. Not that Isovel cared about that. "What did you expect? We don't know how to run a war either. I think Colonel Travis's reading list may be somewhat…

mmm… more practical than your father's. When you get home, you might mention to your father that a usual military practice is to shoot anyone caught sleeping or incapable on sentry duty."

"*Shoot?* You mean kill them? Just for falling asleep? The newsers are right – you people *are* brutes."

"Apparently, if you shoot a few, the others are vastly encouraged to stay awake. Not that we have that problem. *Our* soldiers are all volunteers and totally dedicated to the cause, naturally. So what are your people doing with the sleepers and drunkards?"

"They're sent to the rear for an intensive self-criticism session until they understand the error of their ways."

"*Mm*-hmm. 'Self-criticism' well behind the lines sounds a lot pleasanter than being out on the sharp edge. How's that working for you?"

"I have every reason to believe it will work out very well," Isovel said. "Our entire society is based upon harmony and consensus. We just haven't had time to work with the draftees individually."

Gabrel snorted. "I guess your usual way of dealing with… mmm…lack of harmony won't work here. The army's already here, so you can't threaten to ship 'em out to Esilia."

"We wouldn't do that in any case. Only the worst criminals are deported!"

"Mmm. Depends what the meaning of 'worst' is, I guess. Nearly all the people sent out here are political prisoners. Have been from the beginning. See, that's how Harmony maintains its harmony: just get rid of anyone who questions the program."

"That is not true." Isovel said tightly. "Traitors are dealt with as compassionately as everybody else, by re-education and training. As they join the rest of us in correct thinking, naturally they cease to be traitors – just as our erring soldiers will cease to disobey the rules put in place for their benefit."

"Lighten up," Gabrel advised lazily. "I'm not a public meeting. And *I* don't mind if you Harmonicas are hopeless at discipline. Makes our job that much easier."

"Your job! Running around the mountains in rags, raiding our outposts when you get up the courage? When are you idiots going to give up this farce?"

"The question is," Gabrel said, "when are *you* going to give it up? How much longer will Harmony keep paying for men and supplies when all the army does is sit behind its rings of defenses and send out little groups to oppress helpless farmers on the plains? That's one hell of a logistics chain you've got to maintain – the width of the ocean. And I hear the war's not so popular in Harmony even now."

"It will be different now that my father is in charge. *He* won't just sit behind his defenses. He was already thinking of leading an invasion force into the mountains to put you rabble down once and for all. Now that you've kidnapped me, he'll definitely do that."

"Will he?" Gabrel murmured, an infuriating smile on his face. "Oh, I hope so. I do hope so."

"Do you think a handful of – of *peasants* can stand up to a real army?"

"Well, now," said Gabrel, "I thought we'd agreed that your people don't have a 'real army' but just a bunch of amateur Harmonicas falling over their own feet and getting in each other's way."

"Why do you keep calling us – that – 'Harmonicas'? *We* refer to ourselves as Citizens."

"Um. Well. 'Harmonians,' sounds kind of silly, don't you think? Like an ancient tribe."

"Whereas an invented word like 'Harmonicas,' makes perfect sense."

"Well, in a way… It's an antique musical instrument, see. Doesn't take a lot of skill; you make the notes by blowing through this mouthpiece…"

"An instrument that works on a lot of hot air!" Isovel snickered. She was quicker on the uptake than he'd expected. "Oh dear, I shouldn't laugh… but when I think of all the consensus-building meetings I've sat through…"

"Well, you won't have to worry about that here."

"No? But I won't be here for long. I told you, the Expeditionary Force is probably mobilizing to conquer the district at this very minute. Our people will just have to come up here and pacify your precious mountains the same way we did your plains farms and your pathetic excuse for a city."

"Will they? And this time," he said, looking affectionately at the printer and ink cans, "this time we won't have to settle for the arms we can steal from you."

"Hah! You haven't even managed to get it working yet!"

"We will. That thing's a real energy hog; I'll admit I hadn't accounted for that. Even with sunshine every day we'd be hard put to charge enough solar cells to keep up production."

"Of course it's drawing too much energy. You haven't even cal–" Isovel stopped and pressed her lips together. Had she really been on the verge of treason, just because she wanted to impress this arrogant man with her technical knowledge? That was the trouble with talking to rebels. Traitors. Dissidents. They could covertly undermine your beliefs and lead you into cooperating. Hadn't she been warned about that in the finishing crèche? After Sofiya started talking political nonsense, and then disappeared. The headmistress had called a special meeting to warn against the dangers of talking with non-conformists, and explained that Sofiya had been sent for re-education before she could contaminate the other young ladies.

That local man Sofiya had been sneaking out to see, Josip or Josaf or whatever his name had been – he'd disappeared too; there was an old man running his stall the next time the girls had been allowed to go to town. Isovel frowned. The Committee would hardly have sent Josip to the re-education camp together with the girl he'd been trying to brainwash. Were there multiple camps? Or could Gabrel's claim have been partially true? She knew the worst criminals were deported to this primitive continent, everybody knew that; perhaps some political dissidents were among them.

If Josip *had* been deported, more likely than not he'd joined with the rebels. It would be worse than creepy to run into him among the rabble...

But there was no danger of that happening, because Gabrel was simply lying to undermine her standards and beliefs. No doubt he thought she'd be more favorable to people who'd been exiled for political reasons than to murderers and rapists.

Since she stopped speaking, Gabrel had been watching her with a quizzical smile on his face. "Do go on," he said now. "You interest me extremely. What have we failed to do with the printer?"

"I don't know anything about machines," Isovel lied. "I've just heard the techs talking, that's all. I think there's some special stuff you have to do when you set the machine up, like... like... "She searched her memories for something totally unhelpful. "Well, I do know you're supposed to make sure it's perfectly level."

"Mm-hmm. We've done that, actually. And being on a tilt might affect the production, but it wouldn't suck an entire array of solar cells dry with its first print effort." Gabrel looked ruefully at the misshapen lump of metal that had been the printer's first product. "So. What haven't we calibrated?"

Isovel shrugged. "How would I know?"

"How indeed? But you sounded pretty confident just now. You wouldn't happen to have read the operating manual for this gizmo, would you? Our intrepid traders seem to have left that behind."

"Are you rebels so backward you have to have a dead-tree manual? All you have to do…" Isovel stopped again.

"How did you get to know so much about this stuff? Somebody as high up as your father, I bet you went to a finishing crèche instead of university. And I thought girls in finishing crèche didn't talk about anything but fashion and boys."

He was close to one hundred percent right on that, but Isovel wasn't about to admit it.

"I don't want to talk any more. You're just trying to fool me into giving up useful information."

Gabrel shrugged the shared blanket off his shoulders, rose stiffly and limped over to the side of the cave to get another one. He folded this one lengthwise and lay down on it. Isovel pulled their shared blanket closer about her. The side where Gabrel had been sitting by her felt suddenly cold and lonely. But if this move was an invitation, she was absolutely not going to recognize or respond to it.

"Don't worry," Gabrel advised her. "I'm just trying to find a comfortable position. I think the wrappings Jesse put on my knee are too tight; no matter how I sit or stand, something hurts."

"How unpleasant," Isovel said, trying to copy the tone of her old headmistress heading off a conversation that was veering towards inappropriate subjects.

Gabrel rolled over and lay on his side, propped up on one elbow. Isovel had to admit that he did seem to be in pain, given the tight line of his lips and the beads of sweat gathering on his forehead. To distract herself from the desire to brush them away, Isovel concentrated on the place where a rebellious dark curl fell over his forehead, reaching almost to his eyebrow.

"Now," he said, "what was the subject before we were so rudely interrupted?"

"There wasn't one," Isovel informed him. "I'm not going to say one more word about Harmony tech."

"Ah, but we're done with that subject. Now we're talking about you. It's strange to meet a Harmony girl who chats about calibrations and levels. Did you train as a tech after you got out of finishing crèche?"

"I wanted to," Isovel admitted, "but the Committee said it would be a waste of the social skills I'd acquired in the crèche. For the last few years I've just been running the house for Daddy… and hanging out with the techs in my spare time. I've got some practical experience, but to really understand our technology I'd need to know, oh, stochastic calculus and operations theory for starters."

"You'd have to study those in tech training," Gabrel pointed out. "If they're too hard for you now, they'd still be too hard in the training course."

"I didn't say they were too hard!" Isovel snapped. "But I can't go to the university or even take online classes without the Committee knowing, can I? And they don't look fondly on people who reject their labor assignments. I'm in the labor base as a hostess and housekeeper and I can't figure out any way that either job would require advanced mathematical skills! Anyway," she admitted ruefully, "they might actually be too hard for me by now. I haven't done any math since secondary crèche. Four years of mind-rotting finishing crèche followed by playing a society hostess; I've probably lost my edge."

"That's a long sabbatical," Gabrel agreed. "And I understand it's much harder to learn higher mathematics after thirty-five."

"I'm twenty-eight!" Isovel snapped.

Gabrel grinned again. She had a feeling that he'd been steering the conversation just to get this information. But why? Her age had nothing to do with the technical problems of setting up a printer, and that was all he cared about. Wasn't it?

"How old are *you*, anyway? Having a little trouble keeping up with your crew? Is that how you twisted your knee – trying to outdo guys like Nikos and Patrik?"

Gabrel shifted position and winced slightly. "Damn knee… For your information, I was putting my body out of range of one of your blasters. Into a ravine. It was the right decision, even if I did come down on a slippery rock. Nikos made the jump okay."

"And he's how much younger than you?"

"That's a painful question. Let's just say that like you, I'm still on the right side of thirty."

A long whistle came from outside the cave. "They're back!"

"That was fast!"

Isovel quietly retreated to the niche where she'd slept while the cave filled with sweaty, exuberant young men.

"I didn't expect you to be done before nightfall!" Gabrel told them, his voice warm with commendation. "How did you lay cable and disguise it so quickly?"

The level of exuberance dropped suddenly. "Disguise it?"

"Idiots. Don't you realize the enemy could follow that cable straight to this camp?"

"Well, there aren't any Harmonicas in the mountains…"

"That you know of," Gabrel interjected.

"And we couldn't really cover it up as we went because we had to keep working around obstacles and make sure nothing broke…"

"So, we thought we'd go back out and cover it…"

"Now. Good. Go!"

"Hadn't we ought to make sure it works first?"

"Fair enough. Pat, can you bring the end in here? And Nikos, would you get my pack?"

Gabrel rummaged in his pack and drew out a short cable with pen-like metallic tips at each end and a box with a dial in the middle.

"A voltage indicator!" Isovel was surprised into speech.

Gabrel gave her that disarming grin again. "You really do think we're ignorant hicks, don't you? What do you think lights up the city? Half the electric power in Esilia comes from the dams we put up along the Vanyan River, and the first hydroelectric power plant is right up here in the mountains. Didn't you see the lights in Skyros last night? True, a lot of villages don't use electricity yet, because laying cable and maintaining it is more expensive the farther you get from the power source. We were planning to do something about that before the war." He patted the cable now lying across his knees. "This came from the expansion project. I'd like to give it back to them in good condition after the war." He applied the two pen-like ends of the voltage tester to the exposed wire at the end of the cable, and the needle of the dial spun from "Zero," to "Maximum."

"Okay, it's live," he told the intent watchers. "Now you can get right back out there and cover the cable with leaves, needles, rocks, dirt, whatever works for each area."

"We won't really be *sure* it's ok until it powers the printer." Patrik was looking at Gabrel with big, sad puppy eyes.

"Oh, all right. I guess you've earned the right to see it work." Gabrel handed Patrik the cable end but nodded to someone else. "Nikos, you helped wire Skyros, didn't you? Why don't you connect this for me?"

Nikos grinned, took the cable from Patrik and slithered around to the back side of the printer, where the cave's slanting roof didn't leave a lot of room for him.

Isovel folded her hands in her lap and stayed absolutely still, but inside she was jubilant. She could not possibly get lost now! All she had to do was follow this cable to the power plant on the river, then follow the river down until it reached civilization. It was just a matter of picking the right time to escape. Now would have been good, with the scouts crowding into the cave with the other men to watch the demonstration. Unfortunately, the crowd was between her and the cave entrance. Oh well, there would be another chance. And if this demo went as she expected, it should be a pleasure to watch.

The printer powered up without a hitch. Patrik filled the feeder to the brim with the heavy ink, Amari pressed a button, and the mechanical arm of the printer began to hiss and tap as it laid down lines of steel "ink" in the shielded build chamber.

"Amari, quit trying to peek into the build chamber! The sintering lasers could blind you!" Nikos scolded.

Ah, yes. The lasers that were supposed to bring the steel printout to just the right heat to burn away the clay-like emulsion and sinter the steel particles into a solid mass. Isovel fought to keep her lips from twitching. She was going to *enjoy* this next part.

The printer arm retracted and the walls shielding the build chamber began to glow... and glow... and glow. On their previous attempt, the glowing had died away at this point, the printer having drained the entire array of solar cells hooked up to it.

This time there would be no power failure to stop a disaster.

The watching men held their breath. Isovel looked away.

If they kept staring like that, and what she expected happened, they would be blinded.

Not that she cared about a bunch of terrorists, but what if they took out their anger on her? It was simple self-protection to warn them.

"All of you – look away! Now!" Her voice was high and sharp enough to cut through the buzz of casual commenting. "This machine isn't calibrated; when it fails, the shields will fail first and the lasers can blind you!" *Not to mention burning your faces off. People aren't designed to withstand temperatures that can melt steel.*

There was a disbelieving murmur.

"Do what she says!" Gabrel shouted. "She's a trained tech!" She felt him beside her, his hand covering her eyes. Why didn't the man shield his own eyes? "What happens if I cut the power now?" he asked her. "Will that trigger anything?"

"No. It... just stops. Which would be good."

And he went... where? Scraping noises. The idiot was going behind the printer to remove the cable. Shielding on the back of the printer was significantly less than elsewhere; if it failed now, Gabrel would probably lose not only his sight but his face. Isovel squeezed her eyes shut, fighting the temptation to look.

There was a crackling sound and then – blessed silence. Only in that silence did Isovel recognize that she'd been feeling the hum of the overworked printer all through her body. She turned and felt a bone-watering rush of relief at the sight of Gabrel, whole and intact, leaning against the rocks at the cave entrance with the cable in his hand. It was terrible, it was *wrong* to feel so happy that a terrorist had escaped mutilation.

Praise Chord and Consonance.

CHAPTER FIVE

"So how do we calibrate it?"

Isovel shook her head. "I've told you too much already. As far as I'm concerned, you can go on creating lumps of metal until you run out of ink."

Gabrel heaved a mock sigh. "And here was I thinking you'd come around to our side."

"I'm not a traitor!" Isovel spat. "I just, just –"

"Haven't the stomach to see men blinded and mutilated?" Gabrel suggested. "If only your compatriots had such scruples. But in any case, I'm glad to see you have some confidence in us."

"How do you figure that?"

"Well, you obviously know more than we do about how to run this thing. So either you don't believe we'll torture you for the information, or you think we're bright enough to figure it out without any more help from you."

"I don't care what you do to me, I won't tell you anything!"

Gabrel shook his head. "Now, that's just *dumb*. You've just told me that you do have information I might want, and if I wasn't thinking about hurting you before, you've just put the notion into my head."

Isovel felt sick at her stomach and weak with fear, so she tossed her head and jeered, "Oh, now the hillbilly terrorist is giving me lessons on how to speak!"

"I'm suggesting you think before you speak," Gabrel said wearily. "You must have realized we don't deal in torture, but you might actually have to deal with bandits or other uncivilized people some day. You should have said something like, 'Oh, I'm just a girl straight out of finishing crêche, I don't know anything about those complicated machines, I was just repeating what my boyfriend told me.'"

"As if you'd believe that!"

Most of the men had left the cave by now, but Patrik was still there and watching them with bright-eyed interest. Now he began tapping his foot.

"If you two are *quite* through flirting –"

"We're not," Isovel and Gabrel said simultaneously.

"Not through?" Patrik inquired, too innocently.

"Not *flirting*," Gabrel said.

"Bickering, then," Patrik substituted. "How about we take this thing out in the light and have a look at it?"

"Rain," Gabrel said.

"It stopped raining some time ago," Patrik pointed out. "I expect you were too busy fl- bickering to notice." He raised his voice. "Amari, could you come in and help me carry the printer outside? I wouldn't want to stress the old man's bum knee by asking him to take a load."

As the two young men snickered and lifted the printer, Gabrel looked at Isovel. "There *are* times," he informed her, "when I envy the discipline of a regular army. Chain of command is not a concept that has really taken hold among our people."

Isovel sniffed. "I wouldn't expect terrorists to behave like real soldiers. And anyway, I thought you were sneering at our methods."

"Oh, I didn't mean *your* lot," Gabrel said. "I thought we'd agreed you don't have an actual army. No, I meant a traditional army." He looked wistful. "In Roman times, I understand that I could have beaten those two using a stick wound with nice, knobbly old grapevines."

"The old folks are flirting again," Patrik said from outside.

"The boy doesn't understand the concept of a civilized discussion." Gabrel levered himself to his feet. Isovel thought he was suppressing another wince; his lips were tightly compressed by the time he was vertical.

"You need a cane," Isovel said, standing up and letting her smartcloth pants shake off the mud and dust of the cave.

"Are you trying to completely destroy my self-image?" Gabrel stepped onto his bad leg. It started to crumple, but Isovel ducked under his arm to support him before he could actually fall.

"Put your arm over my shoulders," she instructed him. "Go ahead and lean on me, I can take your weight."

"It wasn't this bad yesterday," Gabrel muttered through clenched teeth."

"Maybe you hadn't been abusing it yesterday."

Together, they limped out of the cave. Isovel felt, rather than heard, a current of amusement running through the group. She held her head high, cheeks flaming. There was nothing shameful in helping a wounded enemy.

"One of you find a nice branch with a fork in it and make a cane," she demanded. "This idiot is never going to recover unless he rests his knee."

Gabrel lifted his arm off her shoulders and sat down on the grass, just slowly enough that it didn't look like a controlled fall. "I suppose you're a trained nurse as well as a tech. Or is that too lowly for a general's daughter? Did you go straight for orthopedic surgery?"

"Don't be ridiculous," Isovel said. "I did a course of field first-aid before we embarked. I know how to lift and support a wounded man, how to treat minor wounds and sprains, and how to immobilize more serious injuries until the medtechs can treat them. After you get through playing around with your new toy you can take your pants off and let me check the bindings on that knee."

This evoked a barely-controlled sputter from Patrik and Nikos and a less controlled growl from Gabrel.

Isovel stood very straight and looked Patrik straight in the eye. "On second thought, your commander might heal faster if a couple of you sat on him and held him down so he can't keep abusing that joint."

"Take more than two," Gabrel snarled.

"That a challenge, old man?"

"While you're cutting me a stick," Gabrel said, "make it a knobbly one."

And before he had that stick, he made a point of walking – well, limping – over to the printer, which was set so low to the ground that he could actually crawl around it inspecting the settings and controls without standing again. Men!

The sun grew hotter. Ravi took the forked stick Amari had cut and worked over it with his belt knife, removing the bark and smoothing the surface. Gabrel twiddled knobs, hummed to himself, called Ravi over for a consultation; with an apologetic look, Ravi left the improvised crutch beside Isovel.

"What's the scale on the temperature setting?" Gabrel called to Isovel.

"I have no idea."

"You," Gabrel informed her, "are lying in your pearly white Harmonica teeth. Never mind. We can run some tests."

And to her annoyance, they did just that, beginning with the lowest possible setting and working carefully up from there. The afternoon sun baked the clearing, making it as unpleasantly hot as the previous day had been unpleasantly damp and chilly. Didn't this continent tend to anything but extremes? Isovel vengefully hoped Gabrel and Ravi and Patrik were miserable, working in full sun with no breeze to relieve the heat.

Her smartcloth garments kept her comfortable enough, but they wouldn't protect her from sunburn. She moved into the shade at the side of the clearing.

Patrik was the first to take his shirt off. "Wish you'd let me keep that smartcloth uniform. Among other things, built-in air conditioning."

"We might need it again. As a uniform. That's the only reason I'm not having you turn it into dry socks for everybody." Gabrel's shirt followed Patrik's.

Isovel studied the grass beside her and tried not to look. Patrik's body was as smooth as Jonny's, but for some reason that didn't bother her. Gabrel, on the other hand, was borderline obscene with that dark mat of hair centered on his chest and running down below his waist. And every time he hitched himself around to study a different part of the printer, his pants seemed in danger of sliding off his hip bones. Well, *she* wasn't about to get all hot and bothered about a hairy terrorist shedding his clothes. If the pants came off altogether, she'd be able to check the bindings on his knee; that was all she cared about.

"Ok, I think we've got it," Gabrel announced. Isovel glanced up quickly and then looked away again. His chest was gleaming with sweat wherever it wasn't covered by the dark triangle of body hair. She tried to think about how badly he was going to stink after this afternoon's exercise.

"Pat, get a can of ink and… does anybody have a spoon? I don't want to waste more than a dollop of this on tests." Someone had brought Gabrel his reader; he looked down at it, holding his hand to shield the screen from the punishingly bright sunlight. "Should have thought of this before. The sintering temperature for steel is 1900 degrees, but we have to get there slowly. After the printing phase, we program the lasers to ramp up to 1000 degrees over an hour, hold it there for an hour to burn off the binder, then ramp up to 1900 degrees to sinter the molecules and hold for… ok, I've got it, here's the chart." Patrik and Ravi moved in closer to study something on the reader screen.

"Don't tell me you've got hold of the printer manual!" Isovel exclaimed. If they could hack the system to download important documents… she shuddered to think what else they could read and what they could do, playing in a virtual landscape of the army's information.

Gabrel looked up at her and winked cheerfully. "All right, then, I won't tell you…. Truth, Citizen, this isn't any of your precious manuals. It's an antique book on a primitive method of jewelry making. I downloaded it before the war, when I was thinking of designing new machines."

Why would she care when or why he'd gotten hold of the discord-take-it book? Isovel stared into the green depths of the forest while Gabrel went on rubbing it in, explaining exactly how he'd figured out the firing sequence for the printer. "When metal particles were first mixed with binders, only the jewelers were interested. They molded shapes – the early binders were quite thick – and since they didn't have lasers for precise heat, they burned off the binder and sintered the metal in kilns. Every kind of metal required a different firing sequence. Fortunately, one of them wrote down her findings with accompanying charts. Lots of charts. I had to skim through silver, copper, and brass before I got to steel, and then there's low-shrink steel and high-shrink. I expect our ink is low-shrink steel, wouldn't you think?"

Isovel didn't dignify that with an answer, though privately she was impressed by Gabrel's creativity. She would never have thought of looking up printer settings by generalizing from a twenty-first century jeweler's instructions.

When she got back, she'd have to tell Daddy to delete craft books from everybody's reader. She bit her lip. *Could* Harmony techs delete books from these old-fashioned readers they used in the colony? There must be some way. The readers had to connect to a master library to download texts, and while that wireless connection was active they'd be vulnerable. Maybe they could just disable the readers entirely during that connected phase? No, not good. That would be noticed immediately, and every reader they didn't get on the first attack would probably thereafter be physically disabled from connecting. That's what she would do, anyway, and these bumpkins were ignorant but not stupid.

It was better, if not so satisfying, to quietly delete useful texts one at a time whenever a reader was connected. Could the communications techs force a connection? If only she were really the trained tech Gabrel had called her, she'd have a better idea what was possible. Oh, well, she would have done her part if she just reported on how the terrorists were misusing their library. People with real tech skills would take over from there.

The first test piece failed to burn off all of the binder, leaving a teaspoon-sized metallic lump that – once it cooled – Gabrel could squeeze in his hand. The second test produced an over-fired lump that shattered at a touch. Isovel gloated quietly over the failures. Very quietly. That big lump Jesse kept looking at her with his lips working silently. Gave her the creeps. If Gabrel weren't there, would he try beating information out of her?

But Gabrel was there, cheerfully running tests and twiddling the printer settings. And after an afternoon's testing, he finally managed to produce a solid, functional blaster. Nikos fitted it with a solar cell, removed one-third of a needle tree and whooped with delight.

"Glad to see you're so lively," Gabrel said. "You can take the first shift printing blasters. I need two volunteers to help you…." He gazed around the clearing. "You," he said to Amari. "You keep the ink coming, and make sure you load the reservoir exactly to this fill line. And Wil, you keep an eye on all the settings before each print run, make sure they don't creep off the marks. That job should suit you, you can do it sitting down." He had scored deep scratches on the face of each dial and the surrounding metal; all Wil would have to do was to make sure the dial and the exterior lined up along the scratch line. Isovel would have said something rude about such primitive methods – but the fact was, the system would work just fine as long as all they wanted to do was to print blasters of the same design with the same quality ink.

Gabrel clearly wanted to start production immediately, but everyone needed a meal and a short break after the long hours of twiddling, testing, and waiting. He cursed under his breath. "Damn, I should have sent half of you off to rest this afternoon, we didn't *need* everybody and his brother holding their breath while we fiddled with the machine. Never mind, but let's be a little more efficient now." With a few words he organized groups for latrine trips, washing, and guarding Isovel.

Nikos and Patrik were assigned to take Isovel to the latrine and then to the swift-running mountain creek where they washed. She had already visited the latrine site, but the creek was a shock; she gasped as she stepped into a knee-deep, pebbly pool whose icy undercurrents nearly swept her off her feet. "W-where do you g-get your water? From the river?"

"This time of year? Mostly snow melt. Some rain, but that's only beginning to get serious as fall approaches. The Vanyan's too far downhill for us to use it as a water source," Nikos informed her. He was very correctly watching the tree tops. So was Patrik, but both boys stood loosely balanced as her unarmed combat instructor had taught her: ready to move on a moment's warning. So, slithering quietly down the creek probably wasn't a good way to escape. Not to mention that if she abandoned her smartclothes – which she'd have to do, since Patrik was between her and the pile of clothes – she'd probably be dead of hypothermia before morning.

When she was ready to dress again, Patrik averted his eyes and held out a hand to help her out of the creek, while Nikos held her clothes out and stared away from the water, into the needle trees. Gabrel might have some problems with verbal discipline, but he had clearly trained his people well. While remaining perfectly civil, Patrik and Nikos orchestrated each step so that she never had a reasonable opportunity to break away.

And if two hyperactive teenage boys couldn't be distracted by a naked woman in a mountain pool, what chance did she have with any of the others?

Of course, they might simply find her too *old* to be a distraction. Isovel wasn't used to thinking of herself as old, but she had to have at least ten years on Nikos, nearly as many on Patrik. They probably considered her and Gabrel, the 'old man,' a different generation.

"So the creek comes down from the high mountains," Isovel said as she squelched back between the boys after hastily drying herself on a coarse blanket and scrambling back into her lovely, warm, temperature- balancing smartclothes, "and runs into this river you've been talking about – the Vanen?"

Patrik shrugged. "Vanyan. But who knows where this particular creek goes? This district is all mountains, creeks, and springs. Having been brought up in a civilized place with street signs, I can't keep track of what goes where in the wilderness."

Nikos, who was apparently a native of that village near the camp, probably could have described the creek's path in tedious detail. But he'd stepped out in front of them and appeared to be suffering from temporary deafness. Isovel concealed a smile. If the answer to her question had been 'No,' they wouldn't have bothered avoiding it. So she had two paths to the river: downhill along the creek, or across ridges following the power line. If she once got away, she couldn't get lost; even a city girl should be able to follow such obvious routes.

CHAPTER SIX

Isovel had hoped that the inherent slowness of the process would prevent the guerrillas from producing many blasters, but Gabrel was disappointingly efficient. Not only did he have men running the printer all twenty-six hours of the day, but he found a way to speed up the work by removing the printed blasters from the build chamber with a pair of fireplace tongs – borrowed from Skyros, along with a comb for Isovel – after they had cooled enough to keep their shape but long before they were cool enough to handle. Each of his men acquired at least one burn from touching newly printed blasters in the improvised annealing chambers; Patrik had three.

"What part of 'Just because it's not glowing doesn't mean it's cool,' don't you get?" Gabrel snapped the third time Patrik yelped and stuck a finger into his mouth.

"They're just, just so *beautiful*," Patrik sighed.

"Good, you can carry the next batch to…" Gabrel glanced at Isovel. "I'll tell you where a bit later."

The distribution of the blasters was as efficiently organized as the printing; there were seldom more than a dozen completed weapons at this site. Isovel tried to work it out in her head; burnoff and sintering times should have meant that they could produce fewer than eight blasters a day, but somehow there seemed to be far more than that in play. At least twice a day someone took off to give newly printed blasters to some other group. Had Gabrel worked out a way to speed the production even more? It was hard to tell.

Whatever he was doing, it was efficient and competent. On most days he found time to rest his bad knee, usually while talking with her. Unwillingly, Isovel credited him with efficient use of resources; she entertained him while he had to sit down, and his rest breaks freed someone else from guarding her. More importantly, it showed that he was able to delegate tasks. Daddy had always said that an effective leader could do everything he expected his men to do, but would do those things only as a demonstration; he should have trained his subordinates to function without his looking over their shoulders.

Daddy would probably consider Gabrel a very good leader indeed.

Between the things she couldn't tell him about Harmony's war effort and the things he wouldn't tell her about the rebels, the war was not a fruitful topic of conversation. During the warm, slow afternoons they fenced around important information with casual small talk, or so it seemed on any given day. It was only after several days that she realized he had actually told her a great deal about his pre-war life in this primitive colony. He'd been and done so many things – student, inventor, and now guerrilla leader. She was envious. All she could talk about was what now seemed an intolerably sheltered experience in primary crêche, finishing crêche, and political dinner parties.

At times each of them horrified the other with unexamined assumptions.

"I'd never have made it into the university if I hadn't had my parents and six older siblings pushing me," Gabrel reminisced. "From the day I learned to read there was always somebody strongly suggesting that I read something informative instead of watching space-war holos, or that I practice arithmetic if I couldn't keep my mind on my assigned readings."

Isovel wasn't quite clear what all those siblings had had to do with it, but she could sympathize. While most of her crêche mistresses had been quite happy to let Isovel sit in the back of the room reading, there'd been a few who claimed to recognize her potential and felt it a duty to see that she realized it. She'd learned a ridiculous amount of mathematics and physics for a girl whose only future was to play housekeeper at home until she took on the job for real with a suitable young man from her social circle.

Maybe some of those crêche mistresses had refused to recognize her limited options?

"And what would you have become without the pressure?"

Gabrel was lying down on the flat part of the knoll, hat tipped forward to shade his eyes. He flipped up the brim to smile at her. She was beginning to watch for that brief smile. It made his whole face light up. "Eh, who knows. At ten I was planning to become either a needle-ship pilot or a space pirate. After that I was too busy for fantasies."

Isovel almost gave vent to an unladylike whistle. "You must have gone to a tough crêche! They didn't start leaning on me and gabbling about 'wasted potential' until I was nearly fifteen."

"Ah, that's probably because they didn't know you well. See, we don't have crêches here. Our parents teach us, or a group of parents with school-age children organize a school to get us out of their hair for part of the day. In my case, with six older brothers and sisters still living at home, there was no shortage of people willing to tell me 'You're too bright to settle for that sloppy reasoning.' After a while I even believed it myself."

Isovel felt sick. "You grew up – in the same house with your parents – and –"

"Alen, Mari, Vesper, Milla, Jimm, and…" Gabrel counted on his fingers. "Damn, I always forget one. Oh, yes. My oldest sister. Alis. She married and moved out while I was still a toddler, so she didn't get as much chance to nag me as the rest of them."

"That's practically child abuse!" Isovel was too shocked to be polite. "How can children develop their individuality if they're always smothered by a mass of relatives?"

"If you figure out a way to *stop* children doing that," Gabrel informed her, "my mother and a lot of other parents would like to know about it. Mom's been trying to stifle my individuality ever since I plucked the big rooster bald to make myself wings so I could fly off the top of the henhouse."

Isovel snorted. "Did it work?"

"Mom's lectures? No. My wings? Nup. But the broken ankle? That slowed me down for a while." Gabrel nodded. "And it certainly taught me never to try that particular stunt again."

"It hurt that much?"

"Not exactly. But Vesper decided that while I was immobilized would be a good time to teach me trig. That persuaded me never to risk being pinned down again. Fortunately, Mom was very generous with the sweets while I was healing. I was usually able to hide some pastries to bribe Milla into bringing some of her friends over to distract

Vesper." He shuddered. "If it hadn't been for Milla's sweet tooth, I'd probably have learned not just trigonometry but *spherical* trigonometry before I was twelve. Now *that* was child abuse, if you like."

Talking with Gabrel distracted Isovel from her own worries.

She still hadn't found an opportunity to escape. And with every day that passed, the rebels were better armed. If she couldn't get away to warn the invading column what they'd be facing, the least she could do was wreck the production line. That wouldn't be easy either; running the printer 26/7 meant there were always two men watching the dials, feeding in ink, and removing partially cooled blasters to the annealing chambers.

Isovel made a habit of walking around the clearing 'for exercise,' and casually strolled past the printer whenever possible. Sooner or later the guys watching production would get tired of staring at dials that never wavered. It wouldn't take her long to change the settings so that the printer wrecked itself. If only she'd let them destroy it themselves when they first got it powered up! She was too squeamish, had been ever since she sneaked a look at that training holo with its compilation of industrial disasters. Probably that had been an exaggeration. An overheated printer wouldn't really melt its own build cage and then melt off the faces of anybody watching. The holo had been meant to scare beginning techs into paying very, very close attention to each step of the process. It had certainly worked on her.

In the meantime... well, she could borrow Gabrel's reader and peruse the surprising number of novels loaded on it, or she could talk to Gabrel. The latter option was beginning to feel dangerously – what? Personal? Nonsense. It was just that they were both so guarded about anything that might be relevant to the war, there wasn't a lot left to talk about but their personal histories.

And there was a bit of her own personal history that Isovel had been avoiding.

Come to think of it, so had Gabrel; every time they got close to mentioning that she'd been kidnapped from B ring with a naked private trying to rescue her, the subject seemed to change. Well, she supposed everybody knew about that, and they were politely not going into the details. But Gabrel didn't know why she blushed every time the subject almost came up, and for some reason Isovel wanted him to know.

At the first opportunity after that decision, Isovel grabbed the subject with both hands. It was much like grabbing stingflower blossoms. Ripe ones.

"You and your men have been very polite," she announced. "I'm sure they are all laughing about the way I got captured, but at least they don't do it to my face."

"Nobody thinks the less of you for being in love," Gabrel said, staring out at the blue valley just visible where the plateau broke off so sharply. "I expect we've all done some stupid things for love; I know *I* have."

It was tempting – very tempting – to follow that up. Isovel grasped her imaginary bundle of stingflowers a little harder. "If it were for love – maybe I wouldn't mind so much."

"You don't love him?"

"I thought I did," Isovel said. "In the last week, though, I've had a lot of time to think… And what I think now is, I was behaving like a silly young girl. Playing at love to amuse myself. It was so *boring* being Daddy's housekeeper and hostess here. I couldn't even go out to visit my friends, the way I could on Harmony. And Jonny was always doing little things for me. Being unobtrusively in the way when Governor Serman tried to maneuver me into the conservatory. Finding native spices that I couldn't go out and shop for myself. It's, it's hard to explain…"

"Oh?" Gabrel turned to face her. "I don't find it at all hard to understand why a young man would go out of his way to make a good impression on you." The look of frank admiration in Gabrel's eyes made Isovel blush. Again.

"Yes, well, he did," Isovel blurted. "And he was somebody I could talk to without all the political fencing and game-playing of the senior Committee officers, and he was sympathetic, and… that was really all there was to it before Daddy put his foot down, said I was going to be talked about if this went on, and had him sent to the front."

"Hmm. If you'll forgive me saying so, your father doesn't have much of an idea how to handle young girls. He was practically forcing you to be in love."

Isovel flushed painfully. "Well. I'm not exactly a young girl. And I – was stupid. I loved the secrecy and the difficulty of getting out to B ring. It was… exciting. I thought what I was feeling was love." She twisted her hands. The imaginary stingflowers burned. "The truth is – I was using him. And I'm eight years older than he is!"

Gabrel choked.

"It's not funny!" She eyed him cautiously. "But you're not shocked."

"Mmm. You've never been a twenty-year-old man being led around by your hormonal urges."

"Obviously not!"

"Let me just say… from the depths of my experience as a man… I doubt very much that your private would have any objection to being 'used' in that fashion. He probably thought he'd died and gone to heaven."

"Oh…." An invisible weight slid off Isovel's shoulders. "I… hadn't thought of it that way."

"And you did say he was incredibly good looking. He might have been using that to influence you."

"I don't think he's that subtle," Isovel said regretfully. "But he is amazingly good-looking, especially for someone whose parents didn't have access to a gene scanner."

"Huh?"

"Well, all of the Central Committee families are scanned for optimal attributes. That's why we tend to be rather boringly tall and blonde with regular features."

"Right. That explains why I find looking at you such a bore. Appearance is so superficial. I'm sure I would find it much more interesting to look at your short, cross-eyed sister with a monobrow."

Isovel laughed. "Now you're being silly. I could never have a short, ugly sister."

"Your parents' genes are that perfect?"

"No, stupid, but any non-optimal chromosomal combinations are deleted as soon as they can be scanned – usually in the first month."

She felt Gabrel stiffen beside her.

"You abort babies for not being pretty enough?"

"Delete fetuses," Isovel corrected his wording.

"All right. *Now* I'm shocked." Gabrel stood up stiffly. "Your pardon; I must get back to work."

For the next couple of days, Gabrel took his breaks with his e-reader instead of seeking out her company. Isovel had more than enough time to think – and instead of thinking about sabotage and escape, she thought about that last conversation. Gabrel hadn't condemned her for what she still considered an ethically ambiguous relationship with Jonny. She'd thought of him as broad-minded and easy-going… and then he'd suddenly acted as if he wanted to put half a province between them, just because every family she knew used gene scanning to optimize their progeny. What was wrong with gene scanning, anyway? Wasn't it a good idea to be warned ahead of time if you'd conceived a child with a fatal disease, one that probably wouldn't live to be born anyway?

But crooked teeth and a snub nose aren't fatal diseases.

Unless you had the bad luck to be conceived by a high-ranking Committee member…

I'm an only child. I was born late in Mother's life; they tell me that's why she had such a hard time with the pregnancy and never fully recovered from my birth.

How many of my brothers and sisters were deleted for not being perfect?

Isovel told herself to forget it, and to start working on escape/sabotage plans. She was *glad* Gabrel was keeping his distance; she didn't need that distraction.

Two days later most of the men who weren't working directly on production went out hunting, looking for some of the native wildlife to give a little variety of texture and flavor to their diet of sludge. Patrik and Wil were left in charge of the printer, and Gabrel had his nose in his reader. She wouldn't have a better opportunity to make mischief.

She walked briskly across the clearing several times before slowing, as if tired, near the printer. "So tell me, Patrik," she asked casually, "how did a nice boy like you wind up in this gang of ruffians? Did they force you to join them?"

"Drafting really doesn't work so well for irregular forces," Patrik said.

"So what's your story? I know you're not from around here. Did you grow up on a plains farm?"

Patrik pretended to shudder. "Farming? A delicate lad like me? Please! Mom and Dad are totally city people."

Isovel sat down with one fluid twisting motion that highlighted the length of her slender legs under the dark green smartcloth. Those tedious Modern Dance classes were finally coming in handy. "How fascinating! What's their profession?"

Patrik shook his head. "Sorry. We're not supposed to say anything that could identify our relatives."

"Why?"

"Reprisals."

"Oh… but Harmony would never hold a man's family guilty for what he did. At worst your parents might be invited to join a self-criticism group where they could reflect on where they went wrong in your upbringing."

Patrik laughed sourly. "Is that a fact? You don't know Governor Serman. His 'self-criticism groups' come with handcuffs and blasters. That's how I got into this line of work."

"He threatened your parents?" Isovel didn't even have to pretend to be shocked. "He vastly misunderstood his authority. But you don't have to fear for them now. My father is in charge and he would never countenance that kind of thing."

"Not my parents. Mother of a girl I knew. She's dead now."

"The mother?"

"Both of them. So I think I'll just wait a while before trusting in your father's justice and clemency, okay? And in case you were wondering… Patrik isn't my real name."

Well, so much for that. As a seductive spy, she was a really good untrained tech. Instead of distracting Patrik with flirtation, she'd made him furious.

Of course, anger was also distracting. She was within arm's reach of the controls...

"Is Wil asleep?"

"Quite likely. He's the laziest son of a... doat I've even known." But Patrik stood up and went around the printer to stir Wil with his toe.

It was in the sintering phase. Isovel reached for the temperature controls and paused, one hand on the first dial. If she turned it all the way up the printer would definitely fail.

And if that training holo *hadn't* been an exaggeration? Isovel's mental vision offered up a vision of Patrik, his face melted off but somehow not dead, screaming... Discord! She couldn't do it. She would have to figure out a less fatal way to cripple the printer.

"*What are you doing?*" Patrik came charging around the machine and tackled her, throwing her back and away from the printer's control panel. "Wil, you lazy son of a doat, check the settings! What did you do to it?" he demanded.

Absolutely nothing. Because I'm a hypersensitive girly-girl. But maybe she could salvage something from the wreck.

"You'll never know! You won't see anything different on the control panel." That was certainly true. Isovel decided to throw a giggle in, and was shocked at how easy it was to sound hysterical. Well, with a furious young man pressing you down, his hands tightening around your throat...

There were these strange spots floating in front of her eyes. "If you strangle me," she managed with her last thin thread of air, "you won't know what happened until your precious printer self-destructs."

Patrik's hands loosened. "Tell me!"

"No!"

He banged her head on the ground. "No!" she shrieked again.

"Dear me, Patrik," drawled a familiar voice, "didn't your mother ever teach you that *no* means *no*?"

Patrik's weight lifted off her. "I wasn't trying to…"

"I didn't really think you were," Gabrel said. "Even Patrik, I told myself, wouldn't be stupid enough to rape the girl in broad daylight and before witnesses. So tell me, Patrik, what *were* you stupid enough to do?"

"I took my eyes off the control panel for a moment. Caught her monkeying with it. Trying to make her tell me what she did."

"Mmm. Forgive my slowness, but I can't understand why it would be easier to attack a woman than to look at the control panel."

"She claimed whatever she did wouldn't show on the controls."

"Ah. A secret self-destruct button? I very much doubt that. Wil, does everything look normal to you? Good. Patrik, let the girl go, she's playing you for a fool." Gabrel offered a hand; Isovel ignored it and stood as gracefully as she had first sat down. It made her feel slightly better about being found flat on her back, flailing to get away from Patrik.

Gabrel met her eyes with a penetrating stare. "You didn't do anything at all to the printer, did you?"

Isovel felt too much at a disadvantage to lie. "No."

"You calculated that it would mess up production just as much if you made us afraid you had done something?"

"Not as much," Isovel admitted. "But…I couldn't think of anything but overheating it to failure and you know what that would have done. I only wanted to damage the machine, not people."

"You see, Patrik? The lady's a very principled Harmonica. She eschews violence."

After that spectacular failure Isovel applied herself to the problem of escape. If she couldn't stop the terrorists from making weapons, she must at least warn the army that they'd not be up against helpless unarmed civilians, but facing blaster fire in a territory where any rock or tree could conceal an armed enemy. The problem wasn't just slipping away; it was having her departure go unnoticed until she was safely distant. She knew two ways to the river; what if she left an obvious trail along one path and took the other one?

An overheard scrap of conversation added a third element to the problem. It had been one of the days when the glowering Jesse had seemed especially disturbed by her presence. Jesse was never assigned to guard her, but on that day he'd had nothing to do but wait for a batch of blasters to be prepared for delivery. Isovel felt that everywhere she looked she saw his burning eyes and silently moving lips. Once, when she had been trying to follow a novel on Gabrel's antiquated reader for over an hour, constantly distracted by finding Jesse's eyes on her every time she looked up, she heard Ravi cautioning him.

"Don't worry about the Harmonica," Ravi had said. "She's Gabrel's- "

"Property. I know," Jesse growled.

"I was going to say, problem. But either way, it's not your place to interfere."

"Not unless I catch her up to something," Jesse conceded.

"Even then. Tell me, or tell Gabrel. I think it would be… very unwise to take it upon yourself to deal with her. Remember, we need her in good condition when we sell her back."

"We don't need that complication."

"That's Gabrel's call to make. Not mine, and not yours."

Isovel recalled that Gabrel had never once told Jesse to guard her closely watched trips to the creek, and told herself that he was completely in control here and she had nothing to fear from anyone under his command. But Jesse continued to stare at her, and she began imagining that she could tell when he was near by the feeling of caterpillars creeping over her skin.

On a rare evening when Gabrel actually took a moment of leisure to sit with her again, she asked him about Jesse.

"He seems… different from the rest of you." *Not all there? Paranoid schizophrenic? Missing a control chip? Hmm, better stick with "different."*

Gabrel had been squatting on his good leg with the bad one straight out in front of him. Now he shifted position and sighed. After a pause so long that Isovel had almost given up waiting for a reply, he said, "Do you ever wonder why so many of us are running around the mountains and raiding your bases in the plains?"

"Well –" Isovel faltered. "I gather you have some issues with the Governor."

"Three years ago you might have described it that way. All we asked for was permission to trade with other worlds directly instead of passing everything through a bureaucracy on Harmony that skimmed off most of the profits."

"Trade! What do you have to trade?"

Gabrel's grin was… not nice. "I see our situation has not been on the top of Harmony's newscasts. Why am I not surprised?" He shifted again, turning to face her. "What do we have to trade? Mostly ideas and innovation. When you think about it, those are the best interplanetary trade goods. Ideas take up even less space than sasena extract and are potentially worth more."

"Umm. It's a little hard for me to picture a bunch of men who almost melted their printer as part of a sophisticated, high-tech society."

"We don't have a lot of hands-on experience," Gabrel admitted. "Harmony restricts the tech we can import. But they've been kind enough to export their brightest people."

"*Criminals?*"

"I keep telling you, they don't send violent criminals here. This continent is supposed to isolate anybody with ideas that the Committee finds threatening. Once you redefine treason to include having unapproved thoughts, well, you have an awful lot of traitors. And you tend to sweep up anybody who thinks at all."

"And your thoughts are so valuable?"

"Harmony certainly must think so, considering how they tax them. This whole mess started when we decided not to sell our latest idea unless we got to keep more of the profits."

"And what was this brilliant idea?"

"We've found a way to make flitters useable in the mountains."

"Oh!" Isovel had known, as a matter of theory, that flitters and floats operated partially by sensing the ground directly beneath them. That was fine for flat places like Harmony, but she could see that there would be a problem in this province, where – as Patrik complained – what passed for "ground" was frequently vertical. If a flitter didn't crash on encountering its first mountain, it would become useless shortly thereafter, because it would sink to two feet above ground in the first valley, would "read" cliffs as the walls of buildings, and would have no way to rise again.

"That would be… very valuable in some regions."

"Valuable! It would transform our economy. This district is the only part of the continent that naturally has water. We've done a lot of primitive engineering to get the water passing through plains farms before it reaches the sea, and we've paid a lot more for desalinating nano tech along the coast. But if the mountains were opened up with decent transport, we could – oh, start serious mining, do a lot more small hydroelectric projects for the villages, bring in fertilizer – hell, we could bring in *dirt* and give every village a set of beautifully terraced plots so they could make the most of their wealth of water."

"Well, why haven't you done that?"

Some of the energy went out of Gabrel's voice. "We don't have the manufacturing base to do massive retrofits. We were going to license the plans to some off-planet mining company and take part of the licensing fee in retrofitted flitters. The catch is, Harmony taxes our sales progressively – the more we get for a sale, the higher percentage of tax we pay. The flitter project would put us into the 95 percent bracket. That's when we decided to hold on to it until we could negotiate a better tax deal."

"This is what you call negotiating? Hiding out in the mountains and making raids on our positions in the plains?"

"No." Gabrel sounded very tired. "We call this surviving. Your government did not respond well to our decision. The first –"

But somebody was calling him. Gabrel rose stiffly to his feet and excused himself. "We'll talk about the war later. Who knows, by the next time I have a free hour the story might have a happy ending!"

CHAPTER SEVEN

Isovel decided it was time to start actively preparing for an escape. She had no excuse to explore along the cable line, but she could learn her way to the creek and back. She started dawdling on her escorted visits, noting landmarks, asking more questions about the topography. Not that it was easy to find landmarks in this random wilderness! She thought wistfully about maps. And street signs. And then she made a point of memorizing the clusters of summer sunstaff that bloomed sporadically along the way to the creek wherever they could find a patch of light.

"It's no good you trying to learn the route by following sunstaff flowers," Amari told her one day when she had dawdled more than usual.

Isovel gave him her best wide-eyed innocent look. "Oh, I was just admiring the flowers. Could I pick some to take back with us, do you think?"

"You might as well; they'll shed their blossoms in a few days anyway, and then they won't look any more interesting than any other weed along here." Amari smirked at her.

That afternoon she collected white limestone chips from the base of the cliff behind the cave, and during the night she stretched out a narrow pocket on the side of her tunic to hold the tiny rocks.

The trail of white chips against the brown carpet of fallen needles didn't show up as clearly as she'd expected. Her escorts this time were Ravi and Nikos, and Ravi was short-sighted. But Nikos fell behind on the return trip, and when they were back at the cave he offered her a hat full of limestone chips. "Your rock collection, I believe."

Isovel tried to look chagrined.

Excellent. When I do disappear, they'll be sure I headed for the creek. She didn't want to arouse competing suspicions by exploring the area where the cable left the clearing, so in some ways she'd be going blind. But how hard could it be to follow a power cable?

Now all she needed was an opportunity to get away without being followed immediately. Isovel sat cross-legged at the shady edge of the clearing and fingered her "rock collection," while she thought about that problem. Fake an illness? She scattered her handful of white chips on the hard-packed dirt just beyond the grass. No. At best they wouldn't believe her, at worst they'd ask Jesse to diagnose… Isovel scooped up a cluster of five chips and dropped them into the palm of her left hand. If these guys would just behave like the rabble she'd called them, it would be much easier; they'd get roaring drunk on that mountain liquor two or three times a week and she'd have plenty of chances to slip away.

Three chips had fallen in a rough triangular shape; she captured those next. Perhaps she could make a bundle of, oh, spare blankets and stuff to occupy "her" niche in the cave, cover it all with a blanket and just slip in among the needle trees and stay quietly out of sight until everybody was asleep. She captured the remaining four chips in two grabs.

All right, that seemed to be the best of her lousy options. She could improve her chances a bit by feigning a headache and announcing that she was going to sleep early. She'd still have to make the beginning of her escape in the dark, but there was a good moon all this week. Anyway, following a cable didn't exactly require superb nature skills. Isovel scattered the chips and began scooping them up again.

"I can't decide whether you're telling fortunes or playing catch-stone." Gabrel settled down beside her with only a slight hesitation as his bad knee took some weight. It was finally getting better.

"How would you know about catch-stone? Do boys play that here?"

"I have sisters," Gabrel reminded her. "Many sisters. At times, I felt I had a superfluity of sisters. They didn't make me play catch-stone, but I got drafted often enough to turn a rope for their skipping games. As I recall, though," he frowned at the chips which she was scattering again, "there was a bouncing ball involved in catch-stone. Didn't you have to pick up the rocks while the ball was in the air?"

"That's the classic form of the game," Isovel agreed. "Not having a little red ball, I've developed a variant. The goal here is to pick up all the rocks with fewer scoops than I used last time."

"And they told me Harmonicas aren't creative!"

Isovel scowled at him. "They told *me* Colonials were backward, and so far I haven't seen much to contradict that. Only tall tales about magical flitters."

"Well, that's how Harmony likes to think of us, and it's not my job to disillusion them. I do wonder occasionally how they reconcile our 'backwardness' with the taxes they collect for every idea or design we sell, but it's not my problem. Anyway, nearly everything your people think is wrong."

"That's rather a sweeping statement."

"Yes, I might not have made it if I hadn't had the benefit of your company for the last week. But even apart from your misconceptions –" Gabrel's grin flashed white against his shadowed face – "the official misapprehensions are truly amazing. Your Central Committee think they don't permit us to build research labs, and that they censor our university and medical school to teach only the basic knowledge that support workers need."

"That's not true!"

"Well, no, it isn't, but it saves us a lot of interference to let your government think that."

"No, I mean – we would never, ever stand in the way of anybody acquiring knowledge. That's just wrong!"

"Oh? Remind me why you aren't taking advanced applied math classes?"

"That's different. It's, it's a matter of deciding how individual skills and talents can best be utilized for the good of the whole society."

"I see. And who decides? Not you, evidently."

"The Bureau for Labor assigns positions," Isovel said stiffly. "It's necessary to keep society properly balanced: they calculate how many workers we need in each field, and they think ahead to our future needs and educate people to serve those needs. Even if I'm not personally happy with how that worked out in my case, I'm also not stupid enough to think I can do the Bureau's job for them."

"What if all you had to do was to figure out how you personally could best use your skills, and what you needed to study? What if everybody did that for themselves?"

"It would be a disaster," Isovel said. "If you let people choose for themselves, how can you be sure they'll do what's best for the community? They don't have the overview the Central Committee has."

"Were your wishes bad for the community?" Somehow Gabrel seemed to be closer, invading her space. If she leaned sideways just a bit her head would be on his shoulder. *Why would I even think about that?* Isovel shifted her own position slightly to keep more space between them. "Wouldn't you be more use to Harmony as a tech designer than as a housekeeper? They can't have many people as bright as you; it's wasteful to keep you in a position any moron could fill."

Isovel could feel her face burning. Oh, great, she was probably showing those stupid red spots on her cheeks that signaled to everybody when she was upset. She tried to channel her last crèche-mistress. *Don't think about what you want, think about what the community needs.* "If you'd ever had to make up a menu for a seven-course formal dinner, and arrange the seating for a couple dozen high committee members who like to pretend everyone's equal while counting their prestige points jealously, you might not think it was so easy. Anyway, we're not talking about me."

"I am."

"Only because you changed the subject. I wanted to know about Jesse. He... makes me nervous."

"He makes *me* nervous," Gabrel said. "But I've got him under control... I think. It's not always easy, commanding someone ten years your senior."

Isovel blinked. "He doesn't look as if he's nearly forty."

"Of course not, he's...." Gabrel stopped whatever he'd been about to say and backpedaled. "Mountain air, it's marvelously rejuvenating, don't you know? By the time you see your father he'll accuse us of substituting an ingenue straight out of finishing crêche for you." He looked at her with a perfect imitation of Patrik's sad-puppy eyes. "I'm counting on you to speak up in our favor and save us from the firing squad."

Isovel tried not to laugh. "You're changing the subject again!"

"Right. Look, I don't know what you've been told about the war, but you need a bit of background before I can explain Jesse. Like I said, it started when our previous governor, Danyel Aberforss, got tired of forwarding our requests for tax relief and took ship for Harmony to plead our case in person."

"I thought your governors were all assigned from Harmony?"

"Oh, Danyel was a Harmonica all right. He was just an unusually open-minded one, and he'd been stationed on this continent for nearly twenty years. He didn't go so far as supporting our request for a needleport so we could trade directly, but he did think Harmony taxed our exports excessively."

Isovel noticed that he was using the past tense. "What happened to him?"

Gabrel sighed and his shoulders slumped. "We don't know exactly. The deportees who came out on the same ship as his replacement said he'd been diagnosed as mentally ill and was, presumably, locked up in an asylum somewhere. Anyway." He straightened. "Our Governor Aberforss, who was as well liked as any Harmonica could be, disappeared, and his replacement – that would be Governor Serman, if you're keeping track – announced on his first day that he had been sent to teach us upstart colonials our place and he'd brought a special squad of peace officers to enforce his rules.

"He brought back antique punishments like public flogging and hanging – good thing he doesn't know much history, he'd *love* burning at the stake but he's not imaginative enough to think of it on his own. He made new laws. Speaking against the state became a flogging offense; gathering with others to do so, a hanging offense; withholding taxes meant the destruction of an entire village. And he had his own accountants inventing laws about what taxes everybody owed. Excuse me, not laws, only your own elected parliament in Harmony City can pass laws; these went out as Governor's Special Orders.

"It took nearly a year of this treatment before some of us decided that we'd rather die fighting than be worn down daily by his oppressive policies. I understand that during that year Serman remitted record amounts of taxes and became something of a hero in Harmony."

Isovel nodded slowly. "That much is true, anyway. The newsers were always singing his praises. And there were special distributions of luxury goods, supposedly sharing out the surplus from the tax payments. A lot of High Committee women were annoyed: they didn't like it that suddenly anybody could afford to dress in smart-cloth. So then the Committee announced that they were developing an adaptive color-changing smartcloth that would be very expensive, and that made them happy. Some of the girls I went to finishing crèche with took to wearing blueflowers in their hair because they match Wilyam Serman's eyes. They even changed the name; instead of blueflowers, they're now called Sweet Wilyams."

Gabrel snorted. "Yes, we heard about that fad and did some name changing of our own. There's an indigenous weed that everybody on this continent hates; grows everywhere, can't kill it with a stick, and if you cut or bruise it there's a smell like a long-dead mountain doat. We used to just call it stinkweed; now it's Stinking Billy." He sobered.

"Mind you, that's not nearly bad enough for Serman. You must have heard about the Dry Creek Massacre?"

Isovel frowned. "The newsers talked about a Dry Creek rebellion. Some of your people tried to throw out a tax collector. Naturally that had to be stopped."

"Oh, it was stopped," Gabrel agreed. "And most efficiently. Dry Creek will never try to withhold taxes again… because there is no Dry Creek. What actually happened, they threw a tax collector in the irrigation ditch."

"Why?"

"Because there wasn't any water in the creek. See, they didn't really want to hurt him, just… encourage him to rethink the situation."

Isovel wanted to laugh at that, but something in Gabrel's tone stopped her. "The man didn't drown; he merely got covered in mud, lost his temper, and stomped off vowing revenge. Some of the Dry Creekers thought they might ought to send their women and children to the mountains for a few weeks, until things cooled down. But they didn't get around to it in time. They didn't realize that Governor Serman had just been waiting for the chance to make an example of someone."

"Did he arrest Jesse?"

"Not exactly." Gabrel's words slowed down. *He's going to tell me something he doesn't want to say.* "They were still debating when Serman descended on them with his entire body of goons." *Something I don't want to hear.* But he went on, pitiless. "They rounded up the men, raised flogging posts then and there, and flogged the skin off their backs while the women and children were made to watch. Then they let them go, told them to run and hide, and… hunted them down. Made a game of it. You understand, some of the men were not quite dead yet."

Isovel found that her hands were clenched, nails digging into her palms. The slight pain counteracted her desire to vomit. *This cannot be true.* "I don't believe you. We – we aren't savages. No one who did something like that could keep power in Harmony. It's against everything we stand for."

"Ah, but he wasn't in Harmony, was he? He was in Esilia, and he was only doing it to deportees and the descendants of deportees – scarcely human beings in Harmony's eyes."

"People exaggerate," Isovel said in a thin voice she scarcely recognized as her own. "They tell atrocity stories to whip up war sentiment. It's happened all through history. I'm sure whatever actually happened at Dry Creek was terrible, but I don't believe in this massacre story. There was never a hint of it on the newscasts."

"Well, there wouldn't be, would there?" Gabrel's own voice sounded strained. "Perhaps you'd be more inclined to believe an eyewitness account from the man who gives you the creeps?"

"*Jesse?*"

"Three men were still alive the next day, when Serman's bullies left and told people from the next village to bury the bodies. Jesse was one of them.

It's true, it's all true. My own people. Worse than murderers.

"Here, what are you doing?"

"I'm *not* crying," Isovel said between the hands that covered her face.

"Of course you aren't. You're just… leaking salt water. Look, I didn't mean to upset you –"

"*You* haven't upset me," Isovel said with a last sniff. "My own people have. How could they do such things? Why didn't I know about it?"

"Don't see how you could have," Gabrel said gently. "Not if your news is so tightly censored."

"I should have known, I should have *done* something."

"I'm glad you didn't. It wouldn't make me any happier if you'd been disappeared like Governor Aberforss."

"You're not being logical. If I had been, we'd never have met."

Gabrel cursed under his breath. "*Nothing* about this entire situation is logical. I'd *love* logic, I can *do* logic. I can't..."

"What?"

"I just – can't." His hand brushed hers and a shock ran through her; not pain, more like... recognition? She wrapped her fingers around his and Gabrel drew in his breath sharply, as though he was feeling the same shock. Then he was holding her, and she'd thrown her arms around his neck, and his lips were warm against her throat and she was dizzy with longing for him. *I wanted this from the first day.*

His hands were spread out across her back, holding her against his chest, and his kisses trailed upward towards her mouth and she wanted more, to be even closer...

I cannot do this. This man is an enemy.

They broke apart and stared at each other; then they looked back at the camp. Amari and Ravi were working the printer. Nikos was lying back in the grass, face turned away from them. No one else was in sight.

Gabrel's breathing was ragged. "My... apologies," he managed. "It won't happen again."

"No," Isovel agreed. "It won't." *It must not.*

I have *to get out of here.*

CHAPTER EIGHT

The moon would be nearly full that night, and there were no clouds in the sky. Shortly after she and Gabrel parted, Isovel mentioned to Ravi that she had a headache and would be retiring early. Ravi accepted this statement perfectly politely, but his eyes slid from her to Gabrel, on the far side of the clearing. "He *can* be a headache," he murmured, so low that Isovel could pretend not to have heard him.

Nikos was a bit more difficult to ignore. He brought her a flask of cool spring water to bathe her eyes, a torn strip of coarse woven stuff to dampen and lay across her forehead, an extra pillow – that, at least, would be useful when she had a chance to build her dummy figure. The fourth time he came to her niche, with the offer to brew a healing tisane out of some leaves his sister thought highly of, Gabrel intercepted him at the mouth of the cave.

"Stop bothering her," he commanded bluntly.

"Me? Bother? *I* didn't make her cry." *I knew Nikos was being too self-consciously oblivious.*

"Well, she'll likely burst into tears again if you force her to drink that foul folk-remedy brew. Just leave her alone for a while."

Nikos ambled off, protesting mildly, and Isovel lay back on the pillows and closed her eyes. Her head did ache, that part had been no lie. She heard booted feet coming close to where she lay, the slightly irregular step that was the last sign of Gabrel's injury. *Go away. I'm sleeping. I can't deal with a tête-à-tête. Like you, I just – can't.* She concentrated on breathing deeply and evenly. He might not believe she'd fallen asleep as soon as Nikos quit trying to help her, but surely he had the tact to pretend belief?

"You've nothing to fear," his quiet voice said. "I've… taken steps to ensure it won't happen again, and to regularize your position."

Isovel's eyes flew open and she sat up, nearly banging her head against the top of the niche. "What in Discord does that mean, *regularizing my position*?"

"The day after tomorrow you will be escorted to our main base. I would do it tomorrow, but I have to arrange for a donkey from the village."

Isovel felt her throat closing up. "Ah – just where is this base?"

"You don't need to know." Gabrel sounded amused. "And even if I told you, would it make any sense to you?"

"In the foothills?"

"No. Deeper in the mountains. We prefer to minimize the chances of an unplanned encounter with your people."

Was that sarcasm, meant to remind her that he was really minimizing the chance of another encounter with her? If so, she was quite capable of ignoring it. "How wise. Thank you for the information." She lay back down and resumed her practice in regular, deep breathing. After a few breaths, she heard him retreating.

Even if she hadn't had personal reasons for wanting to get away, her time had nearly run out now. She knew how to get home from here – sort of, anyway. Escaping from a camp even deeper in the mountains would be harder in every way, not least in that she would no longer know which way to go. Stuff the blanket with her pillows, slip out when it was still dark but no one was sleeping yet…

She fell asleep going over her plans and was wakened by someone patting her hand. "Headache better? That's good. We've got some delicious roast doat stuffed with water potatoes and wild greens. A nice change from sludge – you don't want to miss it."

Ravi kept up a cheerful, superficial patter while Isovel twisted her hair up, wiped her face with the damp rag Nikos had left, and followed him to join the others around the fire outside.

Everybody in the band seemed to have something friendly and noncommittal to say to her, even if it was only, "Have some more water potatoes?" or "Hot enough for you today? Enjoy it while you can, we should be getting some serious rain any day now."

Everybody except Gabrel.

And they kept *on* being friendly and chatty and she couldn't get away and the evening wore on and on until the men were ready to sleep and she hadn't even made the pillow decoy and it was too late to slip out now. There was a fine drizzle encouraging half of them to move into the cave and she'd be bound to step on at least three people. Isovel went back to sleep thinking bitter self-recriminations about feather-headed women who couldn't even stay awake long enough to carry out the simplest and most urgent of plans.

In the morning she woke to a renewed sense of urgency. And she wasn't the only one; the whole camp felt tense in a way she hadn't experienced before. The lookouts sounded an alert for every rustle in the woods, the men working the printer kept glancing over their shoulders, and Gabrel was counting blasters while those not on lookout or printer detail ate a breakfast of sludge with roast doat scraps.

"Eleven, twelve, and if you can make three more this morning that'll make fifteen. Mavros can have those. Use the uncharged solar cells for them. Take these other ten and put them in the place you know of. I'd rather send them out right now, but we can't risk the delivery detail running afoul of Mavros. The best we can do is make sure he doesn't see any blasters but the ones he's supposed to get."

"What about our personal sidearms?" Since the advent of the printer, despite Gabrel's insistence on counting and delivering the right number of blasters to every independent guerrilla group, somehow all his men had managed to acquire the shiny new weapons. Patrik, Isovel suspected, had two.

Gabrel sighed. "Temptation… but I don't want anybody going unarmed while Mavros' bunch is visiting, and even he isn't crazy enough to think he can requisition personal weapons from my group. I think."

During this speech Patrik had been quietly drifting away from Gabrel, to the outside of the circle where Isovel stood. Now the men dispersed, changing shifts and giving the ones who had been on duty a chance to eat, and Gabrel was… right in front of them.

"Patrik. Your spare blaster, please. And *don't* waste my time pretending you don't have one; I'd love to knock someone down. As a purely disciplinary measure, of course."

Patrik sighed and reached back to draw the concealed blaster out of the waistband of his pants. "I won't even waste your time asking how you know."

"Good decision." Then, as he made to hand over the blaster, "No. Give it to Citizen Dayvson."

Patrik boggled. "Say *what*? I can't do that. She's – well, look, Isovel, it's nothing personal – but she's a *prisoner*. An enemy alien," he added, as if Gabrel needed clarification.

"I said I don't want anybody unarmed while Mavros and his gang are here. Especially a woman." Gabrel held out the blaster, hilt first. "Citizen. Will you give your parole not to use this against me or any of my men, and to surrender it when I request you to do so?"

"I will," she said quickly. *He didn't say anything about promising not to escape. Let's keep him not thinking about that possibility.* "But – I've never fired one."

"Another example of Harmony's inadequate education system," Gabrel said, and for a moment Isovel felt achingly nostalgic for... oh, the day before yesterday, when they'd been able to trade barbs and argue about anything and everything. *Sex spoils everything. Even when you're not actually having it.*

"Patrik will give you a quick basic course on the weapon." Gabrel's too-rare grin flashed for one moment. "Being practically a trained tech, I expect you'll be a quick study." And he was off to another task, calling over his shoulder, "Use the ledge over the cave for a practice range. I don't want her burning down the forest."

Hmm, could I melt the printer with one of these? Too late; I should have done that the first day. Isovel had always been proud of her homeland's high standards – government by consensus, non-violence, harmony among all – but growing up there did mean that stealing a weapon was not even on her mental list of things to do about a problem. *And evidently those ideals of consensus and non-violence don't extend to non-citizens.* She shrank from the memory of Gabrel quietly but firmly describing the Dry Creek Massacre.

Patrik gave her the promised instructions, while she quizzed him about the situation. It made for an interesting, if somewhat disjointed, conversation.

"Just hold and aim it like whatever weapon you're used to – that's fine." *Okay. I hold it like a hair dryer. Got it.* "You can adjust the settings with this dial. There's only one for both effect and range because the tightest effect has the longest range, and so on, they're inde – no, not independent, that's the opposite of what I'm trying to say, starts with an 'I',"

"Inversely proportional," Isovel suggested. "Who's Mavros?"

"Mavros Karamanlis. An ally. Sort of. He's built up his own guerrilla band, doesn't recognize Colonel Travis' authority. Now, to avoid accidentally frying your own feet, you've got this safety button here. As long as it's pushed all the way back, the blaster won't fire."

The safety was positioned so that she could slide it on and off with her thumb. Good design – although a little woman with tiny hands might have a problem. For Isovel it was easy enough.

"This Mavros – why are you arming somebody who operates outside of your own command structure?"

"Because we're going to need everybody who can hold a weapon when we go up against your army. You've got, what, two million people? We've got more like two hundred thousand, and most of us can't maneuver in the mountains any better than you Harmonicas. Why don't you try flicking the safety on and off so you know how it feels and – *don't point it at me.*" Patrik's hand closed over hers and he collected the blaster with a practiced twist. "Didn't you ever learn basic firearms safety?"

"I never used one of these things before! How am I supposed to know what the rules are!"

"I assumed you'd have learned the same rules with whatever you use at home."

"Harmony is a civilized place." *I used to think we were civilized...* Isovel shut down her thoughts about the massacre. "The peace officers carry weapons so that the rest of us don't have to."

Patrik looked genuinely confused. "What do you do about greatcats then? Got them trained to wait for a peaceman before they pounce?"

"Greatcats don't come into the city."

"Huh. They're not so polite here. OK, the first rule is never, ever point your blaster at something you're not prepared to burn. The second rule is never slide the safety off unless you're ready to burn your target."

"Harmony City has one million inhabitants. I guess greatcats don't like being around so many people, so close together."

"One. Milllion." Patrik shook his head. "I'm with the greatcats; I wouldn't like that either. He had her practice again and again, drawing and holding the blaster, until he was finally satisfied. "Now, show me again how you draw your weapon, and if you get that right we'll go on."

Isovel slid the blaster out of the deep pocket she'd made in her smartcloth pants, correctly holding it pointed at the ground, and tapped the safety slide so that Patrik could see it was closed.

"Are greatcats a big problem here? I haven't heard anybody talking about them."

"In the mountains? No... the villagers occasionally lose a doat or two out of their herds, and if they can't find the body they blame greatcats. But I don't know anybody who's actually seen one. I guess they evolved on the plains and don't like climbing any more than I do. Though if they evolved here, how did they get to Harmony?"

"And if they evolved on Harmony, how did they get to Esilia?"

Anyway, Patrik's take on the greatcats was reassuring for someone who absolutely had to be out alone in the mountains within the next twenty-four hours. Isovel hadn't even thought about predators before; they weren't a problem in the city. Well, not the four-legged kind, anyway.

"Mavros and his men are likely a bigger threat than greatcats." Evidently Patrik had been thinking along the same lines. "They're not particular about where they get their supplies – or how they treat locals who resist their looting. Now, if you're actually using the blaster you won't have time to fool with the dial. After you slide the safety button off, you can tap it with your thumb to change the setting." Isovel tried that a few times and verified that the settings dial did actually change in response to her thumb-taps. "Good. Let's use that rock for target practice. Start with a narrow beam for range."

Isovel pointed the blaster – it was a lot heavier than a hair dryer, she had to fight a tendency to let it sag in her hand – and tapped the firing button. Patrik sighed and shook his head. "What did I say about narrow beam?"

"I did set it on narrow! The...I tapped until it wouldn't go down any more."

"Wrong direction. Look at your dial."

The blaster was on the widest possible setting.

"On the bright side," said Patrik, "you'd probably have missed with a narrow beam. On this setting, you won't make much of an impression on rock, but you can't miss as long as the target is in front of you."

Once she'd mastered changing the controls without looking, he had her fire at the rocks with various settings. Finally he sighed and told her to put the blaster away. "Gabrel wants you to have this just in case things get sticky with one of Mavros' bunch, but frankly, I don't think it'll do you any good unless you reverse it and hit the guy with the butt – it's pretty heavy, that might make an impression. Seriously, I recommend that you rack it back to the widest beam setting before you close and holster it. That way, if you do need to draw and fire, at least you'll probably hit your target. Even if all you do is give him one hell of a sunburn."

Isovel privately thought that having a chance to be the instructor was going to Patrik's head. Surrounded by Gabrel's men, she felt perfectly safe – now when had that happened? – and sure that Gabrel would be able to tamp down any rowdy behavior at his own base. She wasn't going to argue with Patrik, though; if she stayed unobtrusive he might forget to take the blaster back, and it would be a handy thing to have with her on her solitary trek back to civilization. Just in case the villagers were right about greatcats.

When Mavros finally appeared, in late afternoon, Isovel gained a new appreciation for the art of fading into the background.

CHAPTER NINE

The first man to appear through the needle trees was such a caricature of a holodrama villain that Isovel was hard put to it not to laugh. Long greasy hair, a poorly trimmed beard covering half his face with brassy curls, wet red lips showing through the face fuzz. Dark clothes that looked as if he'd been sleeping in them for oh, about a month. Definitely not smartcloth. And… a very long knife with a curved blade tucked into his sash. Isovel suddenly lost all desire to laugh at him.

Which was good, because he spotted her immediately. "So! Gabrel is a clever man; he imports all the luxuries of home." He leered at her. "I hope you share, friend Gabrel."

"Citizen Dayvson is a prisoner of war, friend Mavros," Gabrel said stiffly, "not a part of my team."

"Maybe she would like to be part of *my* team." Mavros stepped past Gabrel and put an arm around Isovel's waist. "Why else do you keep staring at me, pretty girl?"

Isovel tittered and put one hand to her mouth, remembering when Gabrel had advised her to imitate a silly schoolgirl. This seemed like a good time to follow that advice. "Oh, do forgive me, Captain. I didn't mean to be rude. It's just that you look exactly as I'd pictured a gallant guerrilla leader." She opened her eyes wide and tried to look as if she were gazing up at him in admiration. It would have been easier if he hadn't been a couple of inches shorter than her.

Mavros gave a gusty laugh. "You see, the little lady appreciates a real man, friend Gabrel." He put both hands on her waist, lifted her into the air and set her back down a few inches farther away from him. "Later, pretty girl. First we men settle affairs between us. Then there will be time to party." He jerked his head backwards at the men who'd been quietly filing into the clearing after him.

The man – boy? who came just after Mavros looked as if the Powers, having designed Mavros, recoiled and decided to make the exact opposite: slim and fair-haired, with very pale blue eyes set in an innocent-looking, almost childish face. He put one finger under Isovel's chin and lifted it. "I'm the Angel," he said in a voice as sweet as his face.

She jerked her head aside. "That's a matter of opinion."

His laugh was light and tinkling – and for some reason, it frightened her more than Mavros with his grabby hands. "No, dear, that's my name. Angelos. Perhaps in time you'll see how fitting it is." He followed Mavros across the clearing.

"Angelos Thanatu," Amari muttered beside her. "Angel of Death."

Apart from the Angel, Isovel thought, Mavros' followers were like blurred, sleazy copies of himself. Beards and long, wicked knives seemed to be popular. She wondered why so many of them were carrying heavy native-ware jugs.

"You see, I am a good guest – I do not come empty-handed," Mavros told Gabrel. "First you give us the weapons, then we celebrate our undying comradeship in mountain jack."

Gabrel nodded very slightly. "I see you brought a lot of lightning jack."

"Not too much for us," Mavros boasted. "Any man who wants to travel with me has to prove himself by drinking half a jug of lightning jack. If he's not still standing afterwards, we don't need him, do we boys?"

A ragged chorus of laughs and snickers supported the claim. "Maybe *you* will not be standing after the celebration. Do not worry. I did not want you to join with my men anyway. Now, where are our weapons?"

Gabrel nodded towards the center of the clearing, where the uncharged blasters were set out, and Mavros stepped eagerly forward to inspect his new weapons.

Isovel moved backward, step by cautious step, while Mavros' men crowded around the weapons. When she reached the cave she stopped, irresolute. Being out of sight seemed an extremely good idea; being cornered did not.

Nikos slipped towards her. "Go on in," he said, his lips barely moving. "Get out of sight. Gabrel told me and Ravi to guard the entrance; nobody will get by us."

The day had been warm, but under the shadow of the rocks Isovel felt almost chilly despite the protection of her smartcloth outfit. She lingered just inside the cave, trying to hear what was going on. Mavros was loudly unhappy about having to share out a meagre fifteen blasters among his nearly two dozen followers, and even more unhappy that the weapons were uncharged. "What am I supposed to do with these worthless pieces of shit, hit Harmonicas over the head?"

"They run on solar cells," Gabrel said calmly. "It's too late now to charge the cells, but if you put them out in the sunshine tomorrow they should give you full power by this time tomorrow."

"And what if it rains, hey?"

"That," Gabrel said, "is doubtless why the manual advises charging the cells to the full and recharging them at every opportunity. To prepare against a rainy day."

There was a moment of tension during which Isovel held her breath; then Mavros decided to be amused. His great bellowing laugh was the cue for first his men, then Gabrel's, to laugh also. He continued to complain about the paucity of weapons for some time, but there was no real force behind the complaints. When Gabrel offered to let some of his men stay for a few days and work the printer to make more blasters, he apparently found that funny too. Funny enough to make a seemingly endless chain of jokes about Gabrel's men being workers and his men being fighters. At least Isovel supposed they were jokes, given that Mavros laughed loudly and applauded his own wit after each one. She couldn't understand half of his allusions, and the bits she could understand weren't funny.

After the ritualized bargaining, Mavros told his men to start passing around the lightning jack. He refused the offer of a meal first, saying that no man with any pride would eat sludge. Isovel rather thought that Gabrel's men were too bright for that. Certainly he wasn't encouraging the attitude; Amari, a quiet shadow in the dusk, brought bowls of sludge to the cave mouth for Ravi, Nikos and her.

It wasn't that bad; they had no roast meat to add to it today, but a sharp, tangy sprinkling of some mountain herb gave even the sludge some flavor. And there was some of the local goat cheese crumbled on the top. And anyway, she would need strength for her escape later, and it really wasn't that bad.

Really.

After a few rounds of lightning jack Mavros' men started wandering around the clearing, either to prove they could still stand or to find a nice tree to relieve themselves against. Ravi and Nikos tensed whenever anyone came near the cave mouth, and Isovel kept one hand on her own blaster for an interminable period until the wandering died down. After that the "singing" started: off-key renditions of what she supposed were local popular tunes, with words that were – well, Isovel didn't think that using those particular words so liberally was the acme of wit, but Mavros' band clearly would have voted her down.

Mavros caught sight of Ravi and Nikos and bellowed at them to join the group, he didn't want anyone cheated out of their celebration. "Go on," Isovel urged in an undertone. "It'll be fine. They've forgotten all about me, and anyway I've got this." She patted the blaster, which was beginning to seem like her best friend rather than an ugly killing device.

Ravi hesitated. "Go! D'you want to give them an excuse for a fight?" Gabrel's men were outnumbered more than two to one. On the other hand, their blasters were fully charged and functional. Brawling would be a gamble, one Isovel suspected Gabrel had ordered his men not to take as long as they could maintain a superficially friendly relationship with their undesirable guests.

Not that her urging was all that generously motivated. She'd been on tenterhooks, wondering if she could get rid of her protectors before people started coming into the cave to sleep. Now, as Ravi and Nikos reluctantly joined the "party," Isovel retreated to her niche and spent agonizing minutes trying to punch her two pillows and a spare blanket into something that looked like the shape of a sleeping woman. *Hurry, hurry, before they come back…Haste makes waste; if I*

don't make this look good I might as well not bother trying to get away…
Any minute now, Gabrel will send someone else over to guard the cave…

Finally, she achieved a blanket-covered shape that should be enough to fool a casual observer. As long as nobody brought solar lamps into the cave. They generally didn't do that at night, just felt their way in and wrapped up in their blankets. And on a dry night like this, with a fire in the clearing, most of them would sleep outside anyway.

* * *

Ten steps from the cave's mouth, inky blackness replaced the fitful light from the dying fire in the clearing, and Isovel drew a breath of relief. So far, so good: nobody had shouted at her to come back, and now she was concealed in the darkness. A good thing she'd slipped away before moonrise; her pale green smartcloth tunic would shine like a beacon in the moonlight. Best to be as far away as possible before that happened.

It was just like those tense moments inside the cave: *Hurry, hurry* now warred with *I can't even see my feet, let alone where I'm stepping.* As soon as she was well along the path through the needle trees, Isovel knelt and made sure she was following the cable line. *I hope they remember all those hints I dropped about wanting to know the way to the creek. And don't think about the perfect trail they've given me with this cable.*

That was before she got to the part where Gabrel's men had gotten serious about disguising the cable. Now she slowed even more. Take a step; kneel; feel for the cable under dead needles and dirt; take another step. *At least I'm not at risk of twisting my ankle, traveling at this speed.* But by the time the moon rose she was desperate to move faster. She'd never get to the river at this rate. And she was going to have to leave the cable and double back to it, because here it ran under a pile of boulders that spilled on down the mountain. All right, how hard could this be? *I'm going downhill, away from the cable. When I can work around the boulders I'll go back uphill. It's really not possible to get lost.*

True, finding "uphill" was harder than she'd thought; she started on two trails that seemed to offer good chances to backtrack, but one of them died in a hopeless tangle of dead trees and vines and the next one paused on a slight saddle and then ran back down into a ravine. *I don't remember a ravine coming down. Well, I suppose the path on that side of the boulders didn't cross it.*

When she did find a good place to work her way uphill, it didn't feel quite right. She wasn't going straight up the hill, she was forced to angle across at a slant. Impossible to tell, this far from the boulder slide, exactly where she would pick up the cable again.

Where the moonlight shone through the trees, it lit up every slight irregularity of rocks and earth in sharp chiaroscuro. Isovel stopped and treated herself to a deep breath when she saw the shadow of the rod-straight cable running across the hillside. Several deep breaths. She'd earned them.

After another hour of sweaty, aching struggle up and down the mountainside, she was beginning to wonder if she'd imagined that line of shadow. She hadn't picked up the cable again. Maybe that hadn't been the cable, she should have felt it instead of just looking, maybe it was the only branch in the forest of needle trees that had grown perfectly straight.

Back braced against a cliff that cut off any more exploration in what she thought was the right direction, Isovel wiped her face with her sash and reconsidered. She could keep stumbling up and down hill with no good idea of her direction. Not good. She could wait until morning and renew her search for the cable. Not much better.

Or… Now that she wasn't walking or panting, the small sounds of the forest were more noticeable. And there weren't many of those; a passing breeze sifting the tops of the needle trees, the skittering of some small nocturnal animal that had thought better of investigating this large crashing two-legged invader, and… the trickle of water. Isovel licked dry lips.

She could go down to the creek and follow it to the river. Too bad she'd laid all those clues that she meant to go by the creek. She particularly regretted the trail of white stone chips; hard for anybody to ignore such a blatant attempt at marking the path. Oh well, maybe they'd decide that she was feinting, being so obvious about the creek path in order to distract them from the cable. Wait a minute, wasn't that what she had been doing? Isovel shook her head. She was much too tired to explore the complicated layers of bluff and double-bluff. She'd just have to find the creek and hope she reached the river before anybody found her.

Her tortured calves and ankles protested as she set off again, this time angling downhill in a slightly different direction. She must have gotten really turned around; she'd never have thought the creek was this way. But the water sounds were louder with every step. Isovel thought longingly of cold, clear snow-melt water, and moved a little faster.

The creek was narrower than she remembered it, rushing through a water-carved canyon in stone. Could she possibly have come upon it *upstream* of the camp? No. It had to be a downstream rocky outcrop that had constrained it like this. Isovel lay down on the rocks and cupped her hands in the stream.

It wasn't the most efficient way to get water, and her hands were icy before she'd drunk her fill, but the snow melt was delicious. You could bottle this and sell it in Harmony. Maybe she'd suggest that business plan to... somebody... after the war was over. Right now she needed to get up again and follow the creek downstream... in just... a moment...

She woke suddenly, her whole body startling at some sound. It was morning, and not dawn, either. How long had she slept? She was cold and stiff from sleeping on the bare rock. That had been *stupid*. And she'd lost precious hours... Isovel pushed herself up into a sitting position against the complaints from joints and muscles.

A swishing sound, like a foot sliding over dry needles... was that what had startled her? Slowly Isovel raised her eyes to scan the steep face of the hill that sloped down to the opposite bank of the creek.

Jesse. Oh, this is not good. This is so *not good.*

"Wakey-wakey, sleeping princess!"

Isovel scrambled awkwardly to her feet. At least she would face Jesse standing. "You win. I'll come back with you." She spread her hands out, open, and hopefully concealing the lumpy pocket that dragged her tunic out of line.

"You wish. Girl, you've no idea how lost you are. I could just walk away now and leave you to starve in the wilderness."

Isovel glanced at the creek.

"What, you think following that will help you? Stupid city girl. You went over the mountain and down to *the wrong creek.*"

His words rang true. She'd felt she was going in the wrong direction. Even in the moonlight, this creek had looked nothing like the wide, placid one where she'd bathed daily.

But what of it? Following any running water must lead her to the river. All she had to do was... get the blaster out... and... *Gabrel will never forgive me if I kill Jesse. It's my duty to escape. We're at war. People get killed. Why couldn't those idiots have stolen a stunner printer? I can't do this. I have to do this.*

She shrugged, tried to seem too tired to care about being recaptured. It wasn't much of a reach. "Whatever you say. I won't give you any trouble, I'm much too tired."

Jesse scrambled down the hillside, grabbing saplings to keep his balance, and Isovel grabbed the blaster out of her pocket. *Never point your weapon at something you're not prepared to burn.* She used both shaking hands to bring the blaster up and swung to follow Jesse's progress down the hill. *Never slide the safety off unless you're ready to burn your target.* She slid the safety off.

"Stupid little girl. You won't use that, you're a Harmonica, you don't have the nerve." He was almost near enough to jump the creek. Isovel closed her eyes and fired.

Jesse's boots struck the rock on her side of the creek and Isovel opened her eyes, startled. *I can't have missed at that range... can I?*

"You can't even aim it," Jesse said conversationally, twisting her arm up behind her back until her numbed fingers released the blaster. "You shouldn't have done that, Harmonica. I can't be killed. Your people already took their best shot at that but I lived." His voice dropped to a hoarse, raw whisper. He sounded like a man who'd torn his throat raw with screaming. It terrified Isovel. "Burning in the sun, my back burning, flies buzzing on the raw wounds. And watching my Raychel being hunted down while I hung on the flogging post."

"Jesse." Could she talk him out of this traumatized state? "That's over. It won't happen again."

"Over and over, every night in my dreams," Jesse whispered. "Now I'm going to do it differently. You, Harmonica – now you can run and try to hide, and after I kill you the dreams will go away."

He swung her round so that her back was to the creek, let loose of her and stepped back. He'd jammed her blaster into a pocket. His blaster was in his hand, pointed at her, safety off. *Never point your weapon at something you're not prepared to burn. Never slide the safety off unless you're ready to burn your target.'*

"Run and hide, little girl," he whispered hoarsely. "Run and hide."

Isovel raised her chin. "I won't." Her voice shook, betraying her.

"You have to!" Jesse snapped. *Back to his regular voice. That's good. Maybe he's stopped reliving the massacre.*

"That's how this works," he went on. "You run and duck and hide and beg for mercy until I kill you. Then my Raychel won't come into my dreams again. I have to kill a Harmonica for her, don't you see?"

If you're not going to kill me until I try to run away, then by Chord and Consonance I'm not going to run! "I won't. And you can't make me."

Jesse chuckled. "Oh, yes, I can. Did you ever see a woman with half her face melted off? I did. Did you ever wonder how that must have felt? I didn't need to wonder. I heard her screams." He raised the blaster and caressed her cheek with it, almost tenderly. "Now *run!*" He grasped her shoulder with his free hand and pushed her away from him. She lost her footing on the slick rock and fell into the icy stream. Instead of climbing out, she twisted so that her face was under water. Maybe that would protect her.

CHAPTER TEN

Somebody was shouting. Had to be Jesse. Sounded far away because her ears were under the water.

A brilliant beam of light, round and tiny like a pen, lit up the water in front of her. *How odd. He missed?* A new sound, like a sack full of sludge falling onto the rock. A hand in front of her, reaching blindly, poking her face.

She bit it and heard a most satisfying cry of pain. *If that's the last sound I hear before I die… Could be worse.*

She didn't see the grabbing hand this time, it came from behind her and the first thing she knew was that her collar was stretching, somebody was trying to twist it and the smartcloth was reacting by changing shape.

"Stupid smartcloth!" That wasn't Jesse's voice, she was hallucinating.

The hand let go her collar, grasped her elbow and dragged her out of the water an inch at a time.

"I know you're not really here," Isovel said to Gabrel's pale face, "but it's a really good hallucination. Could you bear to stay that way until you kill me? Because I'd rather you did it than Jesse."

"Isovel. Stop babbling."

"The voice is good too." How had she come from standing on the rock to sitting on the ground with her head leaning against somebody's chest? The icy water dripped off her clothes; the smartcloth was working overtime to shed it and warm her up. She tilted her head up and looked at Gabrel, and he wasn't a hallucination. He was an exhausted man who, for once, looked his age. Or more.

"Jesse?"

"Dead."

She thought that over for a while. "I thought I'd missed him."

"You missed," said Gabrel tersely. "I didn't." He started to do something very like babbling. For him. "I heard the last few minutes, when he was threatening you. I thought he was disturbed. I hadn't realized that he was criminally insane and had to be put down. And he kept moving and swinging you around and it was a minor eternity before I could get a clear shot."

He'd had to kill one of his own men to save her from the consequences of her inept escape attempt. *He must really hate and despise me now.* Isovel leaned back against him. If this was her last chance to be in his arms, she intended to make the most of it.

"Do you think you can walk? We really need to get moving."

Isovel frowned. *She* didn't feel any need to move. And from what she could hear in this position, Gabrel had no business pushing himself immediately. "We should wait until you catch your breath."

"What an assumption. I am not out of breath."

But he was breathing rapidly, and… "That's not what your pulse says. I can feel your heartbeats and they're much too fast."

Gabrel flinched away from her, stood, took her hand and pulled her upright, dropped her hand. "Oh, that? That's not from over-exertion. It's just what happens whenever I'm around you. Don't worry. I do not plan to follow killing my own man with raping a hostage."

Isovel's own breaths went shallow and rapid as she visualized herself pushed down into a bed of dead needles, Gabrel touching and kissing... *Idiot. What makes him think it would be rape?* But it didn't matter, did it? They couldn't... not within a few feet of Jesse's body... She told her own body to calm down.

"I – I really hadn't any fear of that."

"Good. By tonight you will be doubly safe." What did that mean?

As it happened, she had a good hour of sitting against a needle tree, nibbling a piece of the stale flatbread Gabrel had stuffed in his pockets, while she got used to the concept of another forced march through the mountains. It took Gabrel that long to collect enough rocks and pebbles to cover Jesse's body. Should she help? *No.* Bad enough that she'd caused Jesse's death; helping Gabrel now might ease her guilt, but it would be... tacky. Which should be so much less important than evil; but in her crêches nobody had talked much about evil, and the instructors were vigilant to expose and root out any traces of tackiness. She might be a murderer, but at least she could be a *polite* murderer.

Finally Gabrel finished the job and extended a slightly grubby hand to help her up. "*Now* we can get moving."

"I've been thinking," Isovel said an hour later, while they rested at the top of a ridge that looked exactly like every other barren ridge in the mountains. "When we get back to the camp, I think we should say that I killed Jesse."

"No."

"The others might be... disturbed... if they thought you did it."

"What part of 'no' did you not understand? My action, my consequences. I. Will. Deal. With. It. Besides, we're not going back to my camp."

"We aren't?"

"Do you have any idea just how lost you were?"

"I was going to follow the creek to the river."

"Oh, brilliant. Except this creek doesn't flow to the river. It flows to a reservoir. Last night you not only lost our creek, you got totally turned around and headed even deeper into the mountains. We're closer to Colonel Travis' base now than we are to mine. So that's where we're going – just as planned."

"Oh." Isovel thought for a minute. Something didn't add up. "You don't mind letting me find out where the base is?"

Gabrel's smile flashed for a second. "You have already demonstrated your utter lack of any sense of direction. Since our base doesn't have a street name and number, I think we're safe from any more – from any betrayal. Have another piece of nice stale flatbread."

"Um, no thank you, I'm not really hungry."

"That was an order, not an invitation. You walked and climbed yourself to a standstill last night, and there's more walking and climbing ahead of you today. Eat. You're going to need the energy."

Gabrel put another rectangle of flatbread in her hand. Reluctantly, Isovel took a bite and chewed. And chewed. "This is like trying to eat a carpet," she muttered.

"What? I didn't catch that."

"Oh, I was just saying that… that… it's better than sludge." She was really a *very* polite murderer.

Two hours and several ridges later, Isovel was fast forgetting the notion of politeness. "Don't you ever *rest*?" she protested after

Gabrel hauled her up over three feet of sheer rock. Her own pulse was pounding like a demented drummer, and it wasn't just because Gabrel was holding her hand.

"If you hadn't been in such a hurry, you could have been riding a donkey to the base," Gabrel informed her. "Unfortunately, I forgot to bring the donkey when I tore out after Jesse."

And killed him. To save me. Another thing that wouldn't have happened if she hadn't run away. And a little discomfort on a difficult hike… was nothing compared to that. Right. She wouldn't complain again.

Wouldn't, for instance, mention what scrambling over rocks was doing to the lightweight sandals she'd been wearing when captured.

Gabrel set a slower pace after that. The next part of the hike was steep and Isovel had no breath left to make conversation. Even if there'd been anything to say. By the time they crested the ridge and started downhill, she had become aware of the black brooding silence wrapped around Gabrel; it was almost tangible.

The sole of her right sandal pulled loose from its front straps and began flapping and trying to trip her up. She kicked it off and limped on, feeling slightly unbalanced. It was almost a relief when the other sandal fell apart. She might be able to fashion something from a strip of her tunic, except you couldn't tear smartcloth. Well, if Gabrel had a knife. If he were willing to stop.

She wasn't willing to ask him to stop. It couldn't be that much farther, and her bare feet gave her a better grip on the rocks than the sandals had done.

They were challenged long after she had privately given up hope that they would ever reach the base. Gabrel and the sentry exchanged complicated passwords and they were waved on.

This happened twice more before they reached the base. Was Colonel Travis paranoid, or simply thorough?

"Incidentally," Gabrel tossed over his shoulder after the third exchange, "we change passwords regularly. So you needn't bother trying to memorize these. They'll be out of date long before you have a chance to tell them to anybody."

Isovel bit her lip. Did the man have eyes in the back of his head? All right, she'd been moving her lips slightly as she tried to fix the last password sequence in memory. But there was no way he could have known that.

It didn't matter, anyway. Memorizing the passwords was just a way to keep from thinking about how much her feet hurt – particularly the left big toe, which had experienced an extremely unpleasant collision with a bruising rock.

But she couldn't stop a sigh of relief when her feet were on hard-packed earth instead of rocks.

The base camp looked much larger and better organized than Gabrel's ad hoc camp outside a convenient cave. For the first time, Isovel felt a hint of fear that these guerrillas might actually win in a fight against an organized army. This place looked… serious.

Paths worn down to the bare earth threaded clumps of grass and rocky outcroppings between tents of various sizes. Gabrel led her to a smallish tent, its entire front rolled up to give light to a middle-aged man seated at a table strewn with flimsies – maps, lists, what else?

"So this is the famous hostage who inspired Dayvson to invade the mountains?" The man pushed his chair back, stood, and bowed. "Welcome, Citizen. I hope that we will be able to provide you with a few of the amenities of civilized life that may be lacking among our mobile units."

Isovel felt tongue-tied. She couldn't unleash her usual defense of rudeness against this courtly man. She wanted to defend Gabrel's temporary camp, to say it hadn't been all that bad. And by Chord and Consonance, she wanted a bath.

While she stood trying to think of what to say, several guerrillas had drifted closer. Probably wondering why a valuable hostage looked so scruffy.

A very young-looking man with badly cut floppy brown hair inspected her from top to toe and gasped when he reached her feet. "Colonel! This woman needs medical treatment!"

No, she didn't. She needed to hear what Gabrel reported, and to interrupt if he tried to take responsibility for everything that had happened.

But she was whisked off to the medical tent anyway, where two women exclaimed over the state of her feet and applied soapy water, an antibiotic gel, pressure bandages for the worst cuts, and a wrapping over each foot and ankle.

"It's the best we can do," said the tall dark one, frowning as though Isovel had injured herself on purpose. "I'm afraid you're going to lose that toenail, though. Whatever possessed you to tackle the mountains barefoot? Did you expect paved roads?"

She stalked out without waiting for a reply. The short plump woman patted Isovel's hand. "Don't mind Grayce. She accuses every patient she treats of having injured themselves on purpose. Mind you, in a camp full of young men and heavy equipment, she's right about two-thirds of the time. We lose more men to stupidity than to the war, though that may change when your father gets into the mountains. Would you like to wash up now? I'm afraid it'll have to be sponge and bucket; Grayce will probably kill both of us if your dressings get wet."

Isovel wanted a wash more than the ultimate redemption of her soul. "Thank you. Maybe later? I need to, need to..." *get back to the Colonel's tent before Gabrel accuses himself of every crime in the book.*

Fortunately, her companion finished the sentence for her, even if slightly erroneously. "Colonel Travis wants to see you at once? Men! Never mind. Just you come back here afterwards and I'll see you get a little privacy to wash and... do you need a change of clothes?"

Isovel shook her head. "This entire suit is smartcloth. It traps dirt and sweat and all that. It's overloaded right now, but all I need to do is take it off and shake it a few times so that it releases everything it's holding into the air."

"Oh, real smartcloth! I've never actually seen any. Is it true that..."

Isovel shifted restlessly and the woman stopped mid-sentence. "Never mind, can't keep the Colonel waiting, can we? Maybe later..."

"Later," Isovel reassured her.

But Gabrel was already gone when she reached Colonel Travis's tent. Isovel's heart sank. She'd assumed that at least – *at least* – he'd stay the night before heading back to his own camp and the forbidding duty he would face when he got there. Even if he did hate her now, she'd have had a few more chances to look at him, to memorize his face.

At least the Colonel was alone at the moment. And after acting as her father's hostess for years, she knew how to deal with high-ranking men. Didn't she?

Isovel took a deep breath and mentally put on the character of the Society Hostess who wouldn't dream of waiting for an inferior to offer her a chair. She swept into the tent and took a seat on the folding camp stool in front of the table. *Possibly a bad move. It's lower than his chair; I have to look up at him now.* She didn't allow any uncertainty to creep into her voice. "Colonel, I'm glad to find you alone. I'd like a chance to clear up any misunderstandings about how I came to be here."

Travis looked up and raised one eyebrow. "Young Moresco – Gabrel – has already made a full report. I'm not aware of any misunderstandings."

"We may have... a different perspective on events. Did he tell you about the man who, ah, died?"

"I can't release the contents of a military report to an enemy alien, Citizen. But I suppose, since you were personally involved, that it would be permissible for me to reassure you that I am fully apprised of the circumstances surrounding the death of Jesse Barash."

"I'm concerned that Gabrel may have taken full responsibility for that unfortunate, um, incident."

The Colonel leaned back in his chair but kept his eyes on her face. "Since his was the hand that fired the blaster, that would seem appropriate."

"Not if you know all the circumstances, sir. I had put myself in danger by attempting to escape. Jesse tracked and caught me. Sir, he is... was... the tragedy of Dry Creek had warped his mind. He wanted to kill me in revenge for his wife's death, I think. Did Gabrel tell you that at the moment he fired, Jesse was holding a blaster to my face?"

Colonel Travis's brows rose. "Indeed? He omitted that little detail."

"I thought he might. Sir, it is against the laws of war to harm an unresisting hostage. When Gabrel fired, he was acting correctly by those laws. So you see, it would be unjust to punish him for it."

"The so-called 'laws of war,' are little consolation to someone who has just killed a comrade in arms. Captain Moresco has burdened himself with more guilt and grief than any other person could lay upon him, and he is now on his way to tell his other men what he has done. I could scarcely invent a punishment more painful than what he has taken upon himself."

She would *not* cry. "Thank you for your time, sir." She rose to go.

"Wait!" The Colonel's voice held the snap of command.

"Sir?"

"Dine with me tonight. After you've had time to recover from the rigors of travel, of course. Shall we say at 2100 hours?"

"I should be honored, sir."

Isovel left the tent, her face burning. That crack about "the rigors of travel" had reminded her that she had conducted the entire interview with her feet swathed in bandages, her smartcloth suit clogged with dust and sweat, her uncombed hair falling loose down her back. She had been willing to sacrifice dignity for a last chance to see Gabrel; now she'd lost both that and whatever poise she still possessed.

CHAPTER ELEVEN

Dinners with Colonel Travis became a regular feature of Isovel's time at the base camp, sometimes tête-à-tête, more often with two or three of his subordinates attending. The food was of variable quality; the conversation predictably good. When there were no other guests, they dined with the front tent flap completely rolled up, which was sometimes a nuisance.

"Is that done to protect my reputation?" Isovel asked on that first evening when the seventh guerrilla strolled past, slowly taking in the view.

"The thought had occurred to me," Colonel Travis said. "If the gawkers annoy you, I might invite some of my officers to join us. Would that be an acceptable substitute?"

Isovel smiled slightly. "As you wish. As it happens, my reputation among colonials is not one of my primary concerns. And I know that I've nothing of that sort to fear from you."

"Indeed?"

"My dear sir! One cannot spend several years as a hostess for Professor – now General – Dayvson's formal dinners without learning to tell a gentleman from the sort of sleazy little toad who tries to steal kisses in dark corners."

"Ah – and have you had to deal with a great many of the latter sort?"

"Even one is too many." Isovel took a sip of the mint-flavored sludge soup which was the first course. "Fortunately, my classes at finishing crèche included basic self-defense. Limited, of course; very few of us have the strength and reach to fight even an average man. But we did learn enough to surprise and discourage anyone with wandering hands."

Colonel Travis choked on a sip of water but recovered quickly.

"You don't think I can do that?"

"My child, I haven't the slightest doubt of your capabilities. I'm just surprised that such measures are necessary in your home country. It all sounds most unharmonious."

"Sadly, not all our Citizens have as great a dedication to harmony as one might wish." Isovel looked the colonel in the eyes. "But most of us do. For example, there are very few Citizens who would approve the brutal measures taken by Governor Serman, if they only knew of them."

"In that case, it's a pity they are not allowed access to uncensored news reports."

Ouch. Colonel Travis had hit a sore point there. But the principle was still correct, wasn't it? "In this case, I suppose it is. But in general, it is part of the Central Committee's responsibility to see that the news is not distorted by sensationalism and falsehoods. One can't expect ordinary Citizens to, to…"

"Distinguish between truth and lies? No, it would seem not, at least in your country."

Isovel decided to concentrate on not spilling her soup.

On the night of the next dinner a heavy rain precluded leaving the tent flap open. Tactfully, the colonel included three bright young men who were, unfortunately, as well trained as Colonel Travis in giving away nothing of their plans. It was an evening of light, sparkling wordplay; every attempt of hers to find out about the actions two of the young men had returned from, or the raid planned by the third, was deflected by outrageous compliments.

"I can see that I'll have to warn all my officers," Colonel Travis said after his guests had taken their leave and he had ordered the front tent flap rolled up again.

"Against leaking military secrets? I don't think you need to." Isovel stared into the dark surface of the kahve in her cup. "They are depressingly good at that already. Anyway, even if I did find out something about your plans, how would I tell my people?"

"True. But I was thinking more about warning them not to fall in love with you."

Isovel laughed. "They're charming boys, but I'm sure they're much too sensible to interpret light conversation as anything serious."

"One hopes so," the colonel said. "They're intoxicated by the presence of an attractive young woman, but they must know there's no point in dreaming about the daughter of General Dayvson. I place more reliance on that than on their age. A minor discrepancy in age is no barrier to attachment, as you have good reason to know."

"I do?"

"Gabrel Moresco," the colonel said.

"But he's practically the same age as –"

"Ah. You didn't know, after all. I had wondered."

"His men tease him by calling him 'the old guy.'"

"Ah. That nickname came about because he's sensible, cares about keeping them alive, and doesn't approve flashy high-risk plans. He is, in fact, one of my brightest rising stars. One of my objects is to end this war before he has enough military experience to start lusting after my position – although I expect he's too sensible for that too. No matter how brilliant he is, soldiers who haven't worked with him personally would have trouble being commanded by a boy of twenty-five."

"He's *twenty-five?*"

"I was assuming two more years before he became ambitious. At the moment he's only twenty-three."

"Oh. Ohhh!" Isovel was consumed by sheer rage. Her hands started shaking; she put the kahve down before she could spill it.

Or throw it.

"How *dare* he! Making me look a fool! He told me he was 'still the right side of thirty.'"

"Technically true," Colonel Travis pointed out.

"But totally misleading. I thought he was my age or I'd never – never have allowed myself to –" Fingernails dug into her palms.

The Colonel patted one of her clenched hands. "Does it matter so much? From my perspective, you are both very young. And young people, thrown together, are prone to imagining that mutual attraction is the same as a serious attachment – especially when they are safe from the consequences of their feelings."

Isovel relaxed slightly. "You're quite right. Naturally, I never imagined any – any long-term attachment." She hadn't thought about the future at all. Hadn't wanted to. "Given that he's a rebel, and that my father was sent here to put the rebellion down. Those would seem to be insuperable obstacles to any – relationship – between us."

"Exactly so." Colonel Travis rose and bowed to her. "I'm glad we had this little chat."

"I too," Isovel lied. *Well, you* should *be glad. What did you expect? Whatever his age, he's still one of the enemy. When did you start to imagine that you could just wish that away?*

* * *

If Gabrel didn't feel his ears burning that night, it was only because all his concentration was dedicated to listening over the drumming rain for the whistle that would tell him the advancing column was close enough to attack. The invading army's supply train was moving extremely slowly on its first encounter with the serious mountains beyond the foothills; his estimate of when he needed to set up the ambush had been off by hours. Who'd have thought they'd be stupid enough to try and march after dark? He'd be lucky if none of his men fell asleep during the prolonged wait. It was already starting; at least, his right foot was asleep, and he dared not move to shake off the pins-and-needles sensation when at any moment he expected to hear the clanking harness of the army's pack donkeys. And the bush above him had dumped icy rainwater on the back of his neck more times than he could count. Well, at least that kept the rest of him awake.

There it was at last; a distant sound of feet and hooves on the treacherous, crumbling stone of the river bank. And just one hundred breaths later, the low whistle telling him that the leading edge of this part of the supply train had passed his lookout. Gabrel counted to thirty and fired his blaster down towards the column on the widest possible beam setting, where it served more to illuminate the targets than to do any serious damage. Almost immediately, lower and tighter-focused blaster fire shot out of the low scrub ahead and to the left side of the column. Cries of alarm – an unfortunate beast squealing – shouted commands followed the first attack.

Gabrel holstered his blaster and sprinted for the bare rock above this patch of shrubbery. The whole plan depended on his getting across that stretch of rock before the enemy lit it up – and he could not feel his right foot. He stumbled, caught himself, took three strides across the smooth rock and slithered into the welcoming darkness of the crevice he'd noted earlier. He'd been lucky beyond his deserts, and he knew it; if the enemy hadn't been surprised and disorganized, he'd never have reached this shelter in time. He hoped the others had been as lucky in scattering to their preselected hiding places.

Return fire lit up the left bank of the river and the rocks ahead that condensed the stream into a narrow, rushing torrent. One shrub blazed up into a sudden fire that was quickly extinguished by the rain and the dampness of its own leaves. But no one cried out, and while the enemy's blasters lit up the way forward, isolated spots of fire leaped out on the right bank. Gabrel used his own blaster continuously at the wide-angle setting, to destroy the enemy soldiers' night vision and to distract them from those tiny, almost unnoticeable lances of light where his men, sheltered by rocks, drilled into the enemy forces with tightly focused narrow-beam shots.

The wide beam of light from his own blaster began to dim after several minutes. *Losing charge already! Good thing we're all double-armed.* But it wouldn't do to leave his men in place and firing until all their weapons were discharged. Gabrel flicked on the safety, holstered the failing blaster and drew the spare with his left hand in one smooth movement. Three needle-beam shots into the milling center of the column were the signal to disengage.

Unfortunately, three shots from the same position also gave somebody down there a chance to target him. The first shot missed;

Gabrel ducked behind his rock shield and watched unhappily as it began to glow from concentrated blaster fire. *How many weapons do these bastards have? They haven't even brought up the heavy stuff yet and already we're in trouble.*

There was a piercing whistle from well above the tree line and a volley of wider light that distracted the enemy from firing at Gabrel's rock. He eeled out of the crevice, lost his balance and caught himself with one hand on the heated stone, hissed in pain and threw himself forward, half-falling away from his position and, damn it, totally exposed on yet another rock face. Patrik scrabbled down the rock towards him. "Stop!" Gabrel hissed. "It's not safe here."

"Chief, *war* isn't safe." Patrik reached down and grasped Gabrel's arm with one large, warm hand, pulled him up to where he could find footing. A desperate scramble got them both out of the exposed position. They found shelter in the minuscule creek Gabrel had chosen for his escape route.

"You know what, Chief?" Patrik whispered under cover of the shouts and cries from the invading column.

"What?"

"Remember the First Law of Raids, everybody scatters and takes a different way back to camp? Sorry, but you're going to have to share this creek with me until we get a *long* way from the river." Patrik began crawling over the wet sand of the creek bottom, and after a moment Gabrel followed him. Wondering just who was supposed to be the leader here.

CHAPTER TWELVE

For the next few days Isovel made a point of carrying on light flirtations with almost everyone the Colonel invited to his select dinners. Her eyes were bright, her smiles inviting, and her repartee – should any of her victims show signs of taking her seriously – dagger-sharp. More than one young man left the Colonel's tent half intoxicated with half-promises and veiled suggestions, only to find on his next visit that he was held off with a wall of verbal thorns.

Colonel Travis complained once, mildly, that she seemed to be trying to get all his best officers tied up in emotional knots. "Sorry," Isovel said, "I guess I'm just shallow. It's so hard to resist all these charming gentlemen." Nobody – *nobody* – should have any reason to think that she was languishing over that rat, that treacherous liar, that *infant* Gabrel Moresco. At the next dinner party Isovel behaved twice as outrageously as before and wrapped a middle-aged captain of artillery around her little finger. Annoyingly, the colonel's other guest merely sat back and watched the byplay with a quiet smile.

"Lieutenant, I'm afraid we bore you with this frivolous banter," Isovel attacked directly after a coruscating exchange with the captain in which she'd been likened to a mountain nixie who stole men's hearts to keep in her cave of treasures.

"Not in the least," said Lieutenant Mirez. "I'm simply an unlettered Colonial, unable to keep up with this dazzling display of literary references."

"What a pity," said Isvel, and resolved to make young Mirez regret his failure to pay homage. She ignored him just up to the point where she could be accused of rudeness, and lavished attention on the captain of artillery – who did not, she learned, actually have any artillery at his disposal. Colonel Travis had simply assigned him to that position in case the rebels happened to capture any heavy weaponry from Harmony's army. *That* would be an interesting bit of information for her father… if she saw him before the war was over. Colonel Travis had been blandly uninformative when she asked if he'd even begun negotiating for her return.

"I dare say, in return for letting me go, my father would be willing to postpone direct attacks on the mountains."

"No good leader would allow personal motives to dictate his actions," the colonel had replied, exuding a satisfaction that made Isovel wonder if he, like Gabrel, actually *wanted* to be invaded. Perhaps there was a streak of insanity among the deportees who'd populated Esilia.

Just at the end of the dinner, though, Lieutenant Mirez caught Isovel's complete attention. While she and the captain played a game of pretending to be desolated by their upcoming parting, Mirez said something in an undertone to Colonel Travis. Isovel heard the Colonel's reply: "I give Moresco a free hand; even I don't know where he'll strike next. If anybody can guess what he's planning, it would be Renzi."

"The librarian?"

"He and Gabrel grew up together, and I understand he was the guiding light behind more than half of their insanely complicated pranks. I'd hoped to use his brilliance to inform our strategy, but since the Dun Valley campaign…" The Colonel let the sentence trail off into silence.

"He's never really recovered from that campaign, has he?"

"Physically? He's as strong as he'll ever be. But … when we talk strategy and tactics, it's like he's brain-damaged; he just stops thinking. All he's said is that he will never again order men to die for any cause." Colonel Travis sighed deeply. "So I've put him in charge of the Library for now. Maybe some day he'll recover to the point we can use his talents; maybe not. At any rate, while he stays at the base I can keep an eye on him."

There was so much Isovel didn't understand about that interchange. She catalogued her questions while she resumed mechanically flirting with the captain. What had the Dun Valley Campaign been about, and why had it driven this Renzi half mad? What was a librarian? What kind of thing was this "library," and where on the base was it located?

* * *

On the next day Colonel Travis conferred with his senior officers and Isovel was free to locate the "library." It wasn't difficult; the first person she asked was happy to provide directions, and added, "So you're going to do a little reading? Good idea!"

She stood uncertainly outside the tent she'd been directed to until a passing man encouraged her to go in. "Even when Renzi's not there, anyone is welcome to go in there and read."

The inside of the tent puzzled Isovel. It was illuminated by no fewer than three solar lanterns, making it the brightest tent she'd been in since coming to the camp. All the references to reading had made her expect to find e-readers, but nothing like that was on the table in the center; only a few antique boxes. On either side, a roughly built bookshelf held more such boxes.

Could those be the readers? Perhaps it was the fashion in Esilia to design bulky, ornate reader cases. Isovel touched the top of one of the boxes on the table, but nothing happened. Well, some of the old-fashioned readers, like the one that lived in Gabrel's pocket, turned themselves off automatically and didn't respond to a touch until you pushed the power button. She ran a finger around the top edge of the box, frowning: there was nothing to push or slide. She tried swiping two fingers across the screen, double-tapped it, and pushed one finger down from the top to open a menu. Nothing worked.

"Can I help you?"

Isovel startled for a moment, then recovered her poise. The plump, fair-haired young man who'd come into the tent didn't look anything like what she'd pictured. Of course, it had been stupid to imagine that he would resemble Gabrel; the Colonel had said they were friends, not brothers! All the same, she realized now that she'd been subconsciously expecting a lean, dark man, just her height, with black curls and a bad shave.

"Um." *Great start to a conversation. What happened to your tongue?* "I was just, um, looking for something to read, but I don't seem to be able to turn your reader on. How do the controls work?"

Renzi's polite smile turned into a wide grin. "I'd heard that you Harmonicas are so leashed to your electronic devices that you don't even recognize a book when you see one, but I never really believed it."

"What are you talking about? Of course I know what a book is. I have *hundreds* of books on my reader at home!"

"Come around to this side of the table and sit down," Renzi said, opening up a camp stool for her beside his chair. "I'll demonstrate."

Isovel watched as he drew the box close to him and placed a forefinger under the ridge of the lid. "You open it like this." He flipped the lid and it swung as if on hinges, coming down along the left side of the box and leaving the contents exposed. Was the actual reader inside the box? No, it appeared to be filled to the top with a thick stack of printed flimsies.

"I don't get it." Isovel shook her head. "Gabrel had a normal reader – well, not a recent style, but at least it had a touch screen. How do you make this work?"

"You've seen Gabrel?" Renzi looked about fifteen when he beamed like that. Grew up with Gabrel – huh. This boy would never have been able to fool her into thinking he was nearly thirty. "Oh, of course, you're that Harmonica of his. I missed him when he brought you in, he didn't stay long. How is he?"

"I'm... not sure," Isovel said. She didn't want to speak of Jesse's death, so she fell back on the physical facts. "He twisted his knee badly a couple of weeks ago, and it was hard to keep him still long enough for it to heal. It should be all right now, but... well, he's still overdoing it, you know?"

Renzi grinned broadly. "Oh, do I not! Our math tutor used to call him the 'performing flea.' Said it made him dizzy to watch Gabrel swinging from a rafter while he chalked a solution to a differential equation across the top of the board. Gabrel said he had to do some-thing to work off the excess energy in his body while he was thinking."

Isovel smiled. She could just picture an adolescent Gabrel leading his class while driving his teachers crazy. "Yes, well, he's still like that. Were you in the same crèche – I mean, class?"

MARGARET BALL

Renzi laughed. "You could say that. You know, we don't live all packed together like they say you do on Harmony. We had one room at the crossroads for formal schooling, and all ages inside the room. Even bringing in kids from the farthest-out farms by float and flitter, the most we ever had at one time was twenty-three. But Gabrel and I were much of an age and, um, both bored by lectures. We had to do *something* to liven up the classes."

"I can imagine. It sounds as though swinging from the rafters was the least of it. What else did you get up to?"

Renzi happily began a rambling narrative of stupid adolescent pranks, holidays hunting in the bush beyond the settled land, teasing Gabrel's sisters, festivals bringing all the scattered farm families together. As he talked, Isovel could envision a younger Gabrel delightedly spreading chaos whenever he was bored, but throwing himself into any tasks or lessons that engaged his whole mind.

She had to admit that it sounded like an idyllic childhood. Every child had siblings and adults who took a personal interest in him, instead of crèche mothers who had to treat all the children exactly alike. And clearly the boys had enjoyed much more freedom than she'd had in her crèche. Isovel had been shocked when she first learned how Gabrel had been brought up, but now she was beginning to see there were some advantages to the Esilian approach. Traveling miles by flitter, unsupervised by adults, just to get to school. Families who actually knew what you were learning, and why, and who brought you up sharp when you were slacking off, instead of just sending tepid approval of your test scores. Adventures ranging from hunting greatcats to evading older sisters who'd caught you eavesdropping on their swains. Isovel sighed. She'd never had an adventure before her brief affair with Jonny Kelso, and that hadn't exactly turned out well, had it?

Renzi misinterpreted her sigh. "Sorry, I didn't mean to go on and on at you. It's just that sometimes – well, one grows up. One has real work to do. But I never had so much *fun* as during those years with Gabrel. But you're not here to listen to tales of an Esilian childhood."

Oh, yes, I am. But talking about Gabrel, drawing out stories about him, was a dangerous indulgence. She'd been a fool to start this. She would never see him again; the sooner she forgot all about him, the better. She could start now. Isovel forced herself to pay attention to Renzi's instructions.

"You see, it's just like an e-reader. You start reading at the top of the page."

Obediently Isovel followed Renzi's pointing finger to a line of text in archaic spelling. "When in the course of human events it becomes necessary for one people to dissolve the political bonds..." She looked up. "Is this what your Governor Aberforss sent to Harmony? No wonder the Central Committee thought he was insane!" The page was littered with words and phrases that were practically encouraging the worst sort of Discord: unalienable rights, the consent of the governed, the right of the people...

"No, this was written centuries ago. We're not the first people who desired to dissolve the bonds which had connected us with another."

"To rebel."

"To demand freedom."

Isovel skimmed down to the bottom of the page. "What an odd document. It just stops in the middle of a sentence. Or.... Can I scroll down?" She brushed her fingers along the flimsy. Nothing happened.

"Not like that." Renzi sounded as if he was restraining a laugh. "Look, you turn the page like this." He pinched the right side of the flimsy between thumb and forefinger and lifted gently. The right edge of the printed flimsy rose up; then, as Renzi guided it, the whole flimsy fell over the box cover on the left to reveal a new page.

"Oh, my. And you have to do that over and over? What a nuisance. And how do you adjust the text size?"

"You don't," Renzi informed her.

"Well!" She bit back the words "What a bad design," and substituted, "It all seems very inconvenient. I really prefer my e-reader." She looked over the crowded bookshelf. "Aren't these things heavy as well as not being very user-friendly? Why on earth did you bother with this system?"

"You can't read this document on your e-reader," Renzi told her.

"Well, of course I can't, it's at home."

"Doesn't matter. No matter how many Harmonica readers you check, you won't find the Declaration of Independence on them."

"No? But I can always download it."

"That," Renzi said with his arms folded, "you cannot do. It *does not exist* on any data base controlled by the Central Committee." He went on to tell her a long and, frankly, improbable story about how early deportees had discovered that the books which had inspired their dissent were being sucked off their e-readers and erased from the data base. "We – they – immediately disabled the 'net connections on their readers. We didn't lose very much… well, we don't *think* we lost very much. About half of Hobbes's *Leviathan*, and some of Plato's *Republic* – could have been worse, given what remains of the *Republic*." He sniffed. "Philosopher-kings. Censorship. It might have been a design for Harmony's government, surprising they tried to delete it. But I suppose they just went after anything dissidents had been reading, without bothering to understand it."

The creation of these printed books had been one of the earliest projects of the deportees. They'd stolen the first governor's 2D printer, which was really designed only for printing regulations and short memoranda, and had put years into secretively printing the books they valued most – learning obsolete arts like bookbinding along the way – just to be sure that no government could stealthily edit or erase these books.

"What if someone steals or burns your precious books?" Isovel asked. If the Central Committee knew about this stash of forbidden writings, they'd surely destroy it as soon as the war was over.

"Redundancy." Renzi grinned. "Did you miss the part where we printed multiple copies of every book? The university has five sets distributed around the campus. Every public library has a set, every one-room schoolhouse has a set. And there are more sets in secret locations. Even Stinking Billy would have trouble finding *all* the copies. And anyway, he's too stupid to recognize that you can make war with ideas. He wouldn't understand that these are our most powerful weapons." He patted the stack of books at his elbow. "So go ahead, read as much as you want to. And if there's anything you'd like to discuss, talk to me or anybody else you choose; these are in the basic curriculum for secondary school, so we've all read them."

He left Isovel to read, and she stayed in the tent until her eyes began to burn and her head was swimming. The Esilians' prized texts were such an *odd* mixture; common sense on one page led to outrageous opinions on the next. They made frequent reference to something they called "natural law," but didn't seem to have any way of enforcing it. Harmony's system of consensus, with self-criticism sessions for those who had wrong ideas, was vastly superior to some kind of "natural law" that was never defined and held no penalties. Wasn't it?

In mid-afternoon Renzi poked his head into the tent. "Still reading? You must like our library."

"Don't get too excited," Isovel said, stretching. "I haven't had anything to read since your terrorists kidnapped me. At this point I'd probably read *Princess Paulina's Prince* if you had a copy."

Renzi looked worried. "Really? Gabrel must have changed. I'd have thought he would be only too happy to let you use his e-reader."

Isovel remembered the last three sentimental novels she'd enjoyed on Gabrel's reader, and blushed to her eyebrows. Bad enough to be caught lying, but if Renzi knew what junk fiction she'd been reading…. Wait a minute. The novels had already been on the reader; Gabrel hadn't downloaded those or anything else for her benefit. Her lips twitched. Well, well. The rough, tough terrorist had a taste for happily-ever-stories.

Not that it mattered, since she'd probably never see him again.

CHAPTER THIRTEEN

Private Wever was unhappy.

Not that that differentiated him from the other two hundred and nineteen privates in the leading column. He knew that. But *his* blisters, and *his* aching legs, and *his* anxiety were bothering him a lot more than the problems of the other guys.

He felt as if he'd been trudging uphill forever. He told himself not to exaggerate; it had only been three days since the float had stopped and his platoon had been told, "You walk from here." Walk, ha! Walk, wade, scramble, climb along this eternal river splashing down from the high snow-capped mountains. What a barbaric place. Must be two hundred years since the colony was established, and here in the mountains they still didn't have proper roads.

And it had been three long, wet days. The uniform kept his body dry and even stretched out to form a hood that covered his head, but his socks were not smartcloth; somebody in Purchasing had been cheated, or more likely, had pocketed the difference between socks knitted of smartcloth fiber and ordinary wool socks. And *he* was paying for the difference now, squelching along in flooded boots and probably acquiring new blisters with every step.

He jumped at a hooting noise and saw a white shape out of the corner of his eye, then relaxed as the noisemaker ruffled white feathers and flew off.

"Thought it was the White Woman, didn't you?" his buddy Sulivan teased.

"Of course not. That's just a local superstition. Civilized people don't believe that malarkey." The story had spread among the ranks during their march. The mountains were said to be haunted by a woman dressed in white whose wailing cry portended the death of someone nearby.

"Yeah, well, I'm beginning to feel less civilized all the time." Sulivan shifted the weight of his pack. "With every meal of healthful nanosludge I can feel myself going more barbarian. I'm starting to dream about real food. The White Woman can visit for all I care, if she brings some decent chow along with her."

They hadn't been told exactly why the supply train had been delayed. Rumors ran from 'typical incompetence' to 'massacred in cold blood by people you can't see until they slip out of the trees to kill you.' Wever vastly preferred the first version, and kept telling himself that the first rule of evaluating information was, 'Never attribute to malice that which can be explained by incompetence.'

But their general, Rauf Dayvson, was supposed to be extremely competent, for all he'd been hauled away from his beloved history books to invent an army. And Wever found himself studying the shadows between the spiky needle trees more closely than a perfectly confident man would.

"What d'you think happened to Taldi?" Their tent had been missing one man last night.

"Womanizing? He'll be back tonight boasting of his conquests."

"What conquests? There aren't any women here for him to harass." Wever hated Taldi's swaggering, boastful manner. All the same, he didn't *like* people disappearing like that.

"Maybe he slept with the White Woman."

Wever fought an involuntary shiver. "Sleeping with the White Woman" sounded like a euphemism for death. "I'm gonna wring out my socks," he decided abruptly. "Catch you later."

Sulivan trudged on ahead while Wever sat on a nice wet rock – at least his smartcloth uniform protected him from that – unlaced his boots, wrung approximately half the river out of his socks, and put them back on. Damp but not squelchy was at least some improvement.

When they halted for the night, Taldi was missing from their tent again.

So was Sulivan.

Sleeping with the White Woman?

* * *

"You'll never be able to conquer our army," Isovel told Colonel Travis. "You can send little groups of men out to harass and kill, but you simply haven't enough people to stand up to a full army. Unless you want a permanent occupying army, you'd be wise to make whatever terms you can."

"I don't recall appointing you as my military adviser, young lady."

She wasn't seriously trying to change the colonel's mind. She just wanted to plant doubt and despondency in the minds of his dinner guests that evening, Lieutenant Mirez and Captain… somebody.

"Think about it. Harmony has *two million* Citizens. What's your population? A couple of hundred thousand? There's no way you can field enough soldiers to survive a pitched battle. You don't even have artillery."

Captain Whoever was looking gloomy. Then the insufferable Lieutenant Mirez piped up. "We don't have to – oh, sorry, sir." The captain was glaring at him. "You were going to say?"

"Nothing," said the captain loftily. "We don't have to pay heed to the babblings of a foreign spy. And a girl at that."

The colonel spoke up. "Might I remind you – all three of you – that we also don't have to defeat Harmony in a pitched battle. All we have to do is drag this out and make this war unprofitable and unpopular. The Central Committee will let Esilia go rather than risk losing power to a rebellion at home."

"That's what I was going to say," Mirez muttered under his breath. Isovel felt a rare moment of sympathy with him. She knew exactly what it was like to have one's ideas squelched or appropriated by a superior. That described ninety percent of her interactions with her father. She decided to change the subject.

"There's something I've been wanting to ask you, Colonel."

"What, asking instead of telling? What a refreshing change."

Isovel colored at the teasing but went on, "You have people coming in from the field with reports nearly every day, but all I ever hear about is terrorizing our soldiers and picking them off one at a time. Don't most – ah – revolutionary forces also attack infrastructure?"

"You mean, like breaking the solar power plants on the plains, or the hydroelectric generators along the river, or degrading the irrigation system."

Well, at least she didn't have to worry that she'd given him ideas; obviously they'd already begun discussing infrastructure targets.

"Well – yes. Wouldn't any of those have more impact than merely harassing our forces?"

Colonel Travis smiled. "Doubtless they would, in the short term. But in the long term, that's our infrastructure you're talking about, and we want to be able to use it after the war."

"Whereas soldiers from Harmony are –"

"Expendable. Yes. We don't need *them*."

Sometimes the colonel's smile made Isovel think of a hungry greatcat. He didn't look like a kindly middle-aged man at all.

* * *

Rauf Dayvson gathered the reins of his donkey in one hand and frowned at the rain-soaked flimsies his aide-de-camp had brought him.

"You say these are turning up all along the column? How do you know that?"

"Enough men have handed them over to show me that they've been distributed the length of the column. I do not, of course, know how many men have picked one up and *not* brought it to one of the officers."

"One would hope that the answer is 'None.'" Andrus, the political officer, sniffed disdainfully. "I have never seen anything so flagrantly anti-harmony. Even the grunts must realize that something like this is forbidden literature."

Rauf gave the man a sour look. He loathed having to bring Andrus with him, knowing that he was reporting back to Harmony independently and that his principal task was to see that no one on Rauf's staff did or said anything that could be construed as anti-harmony. Around these creatures of the Central Committee he felt that he had to pick all his words very carefully. It was like walking on eggshells, trying to work with his officers while all of them – himself included – had to be as concerned with not offending the political officer as with their real job of winning the war.

Rauf believed with all his heart in the basic principles of Harmony. He knew that he was doing the right thing here, fighting to bring these erring people back into Consonance. But how had these principles led to his own people spying on one another, and everybody terrified of accidentally saying something that could be considered seditious? Something had gone badly wrong. When this little war was over, he'd have to get together with his friends back home and figure out how to get his country back to honoring standards in the spirit as well as in the letter, instead of fomenting suspicion and distrust.

"We don't exactly have the usual bars to dissidence," he pointed out. "What are you going to do if you catch a soldier reading one of these leaflets? Send him to Esilia? He's already here."

"Anybody who's caught with one of these things should be sent back to the city, to the stockade you built," Andrus said, tight-lipped.

Rauf snorted. "So for every grunt who picks up one of these out of curiosity, I'm to lose three – that man and the two detailed to escort him? Do you *want* this expedition to fail?"

"Better a military failure than the degradation of our principles."

Oh, well. There was a limit to how long an honest man could tiptoe around this political malarkey. Rauf leaned forward from his seat on the donkey and hooked his finger into the man's collar. "Listen to me, Andrus, and listen carefully. *My daughter* is somewhere in these mountains. I *will* take the war to these cowards who hide in the hills, and I *will* rescue my daughter. And heaven help anybody who interferes with me."

Andrus was purple with rage when Rauf released him. "Do you put your personal desires above the principles of harmony?"

"I believe that in this matter they are aligned," Rauf said. "I've been charged with bringing these mistaken people back into consonance with the Way of Harmony, and they will be much more inclined to the Way after I've thrashed the grubby terrorist bands who infest these hills. Most of the common people will doubtless be grateful to be rid of the parasites, and those who don't will at least have a better understanding of what happens to those who resist Harmony. To do this I need a strong, confident army. You – will – *not* start witch hunts that will further demoralize my soldiers. Is that understood?"

"When the Central Committee hears of this –" Andrus began.

Dayvson gave him a tight-lipped smile. "The Central Committee, Andrus, is half a continent and an ocean away, and I am right here. Furthermore, these hills are blocking our communications. With luck, we'll take a high point from which we can at least communicate with the coast. If you are *very* lucky, you'll still be with us when we reach that point."

And once he reports, I'll be withdrawn in disgrace, to be replaced by some politically correct fool who will never find my Isovel. Should Andrus meet with a fatal accident on the march? Maybe the enemy snipers will take care of my problem.

But he didn't take the rebel propaganda lightly, no matter what he said to Andrus. As they rode forward, he glanced down at the flimsy. It began by twitting the grunts on their continuing mysterious losses, implied that the officers didn't care how many of them died, and finally offered a grant of land to any soldier who defected to their side.

Dayvson knew all too well that many of his draftees were the dregs of Harmony – lazy, poor, and ignorant. The Central Committee had begun by drafting the people that Harmony could well do without. How many of them would have their heads turned by the prospect of becoming landowners? Would they understand that owning land was not wealth, only a pathway to better circumstances through hard work?

And Discord take it, how many of them would get that far and reason that they were working just that hard in the army with no prospect of anything but their monthly pay?

He shook his head. He knew that everyone was better off under Harmony's system of sharing, where no one starved and no one accumulated excess wealth, than under Esilia's selfish system where the people who were successful thought themselves entitled to keep the fruits of that success. But then, he had the benefit of a university education. He wasn't sure how he would explain the point to a grunt with limited horizons and little education.

The real trouble, he decided, was that Governor Aberforss had spent a generation allowing the exiles so much autonomy that they'd been able to entrench their selfishness in the economy. If that man had been paying proper attention to the internal workings of the colony, this notion of private property would have been nipped in the bud.

And he wouldn't be worrying about their false ideas seducing his grunts.

* * *

In Harmony City, the members of the Central Committee watched a depressing series of vids interspersed with a few even more depressing holos. The people weren't rioting – quite – but they were taking to the streets in sullen crowds. Masked protestors had wrecked a recruiting center and draft office in the old city. Women with scarves tied around their heads and over their faces waved signs saying things like "FOOD IS BETTER THAN WAR" and "BRING BACK OUR SONS."

"Tell me these vids aren't going out on the news channels," the head of the committee grunted at the Minister for Truth.

"Sir, we *got* these from the news channels. Naturally they turned them over to us immediately; they've no ambition to broadcast such seditious garbage."

"But did they keep copies for themselves?"

"Everything the news channels broadcast has to be approved by my office," the Minister for Truth reminded him, hoping the evasion wouldn't be noticed. How was he to know what the newsers were hiding? A single three-inch data slip could hold everything they were watching and several hundred more hours of vids, and the slender black slips could be concealed anywhere.

"Good. Tell them to run some lightweight holoseries – romance, comedy – and then repeat the public service announcements." The Head sighed. "I wish Dayvson would transmit some holos of our victories over the traitor colonists. He does not seem to appreciate the importance of the right kind of news. The city never had this much trouble when we were showing how Governor Serman handled the rebels. Military, please convey our concerns to the general."

The new head of the newly created Bureau for Military Affairs said nervously, "Naturally we shall do so at our earliest opportunity, sir. At the moment General Dayvson is leading an expeditionary force against the rebels entrenched in the eastern mountains, and communications with that area are not reliable."

"Oh? Well, let's hope he took some newsers to record his victories, then." The bald head swiveled back to the Minister for Truth. "Tell the newsers to explain in their own words that we can't afford to maintain the usual generous rations while we're spending so much to support bringing the Colony back into line. I'll write the text and send it out to them after this meeting. Security, what do you have to say for yourself?"

The Acting Minister for Security surreptitiously wiped clammy hands on his trousers. His predecessor had been abruptly removed from office for failure to stop the sullen crowds from gathering in the streets, and he had no tools with which to do better.

"All healthy peace officers under fifty are overseas, serving in the army. With what we've got left –"*old guys and cripples*" – we cannot support the kind of violent response that these dissidents deserve. I've instructed the remaining peace officers to keep their weapons holstered. They are attempting to use tanglesticks to stop the movement of the mob." And it wasn't working.

"Perhaps you should be less merciful."

"We can't kill the entire population of the city!"

The Head fixed a baleful glare upon him. "Are you implying that the entire city is rising against us, Security?"

"No, sir! But –"

The Minister for Labor stirred. "The loss of so many working Citizens would be disastrous for our economy. I must respectfully petition that Security delete as few as possible. We'll have to find some other way to whip them back into line."

"Unfortunate," the Head mused, "that the threat of deportation is not currently available to us. They know we won't deport traitors who would only join the rebels, and that's emboldened them." For some reason, playing on citizens' fear of the unknown was more effective than killing dissidents outright.

The Minister for Health coughed. "We may have come up with a solution for that problem, sir."

"What," the Head said with a dry, rustling laugh, "you've discovered another continent where we can dump traitors?"

Red spots appeared on her cheeks. "No, sir, but we may have an alternative to deportation. Recent medical treatments for the clinically insane have produced some interesting results. We have imported a new drug that changes brain activity to cut down violence."

"What good will that do?"

"Used in isolation? None. But when it's combined with some of our existing treatments, there are some interesting side effects. Subjects given Anti-V after a treatment of Truth-D and a sedative show greatly reduced brain activity not only in the areas responsible for violence, but also in volition and general memory. If I may demonstrate?" She produced a data slip.

"By all means." The Head glanced at the Visual Aids Operator, who removed the slip of recent street vids and substituted the one that the Minister for Health offered him.

"As you see," the minister said as a shambling creature in the vid obeyed commands to sit, stand, and jump, "the product is quite passive but responds well to simple orders. This is practically a miracle drug suite, sir! It can transform dissidents into useful, if low-level, workers. There should also be substantial cost savings, depending on how the Bureau for Labor decides to allocate the new workers; they need not be paid, and can subsist on sludge."

"And seeing the transformation of their former leaders should seriously discourage the other dissidents," the Head concluded. "I like it, Health. But are you certain the effect is not reversible? A lot of the savings would be destroyed if we had to continue treating the subjects with an imported drug."

"Sir, initial tests indicate that large areas of the brain are simply destroyed." The Minister for Health paused. "Unfortunately, since the subjects we were allotted for this test had been arrested for choofing, it's possible that choof and other illegal drugs prepared the subjects' brains for maximal response."

"Well, try it out on somebody who's clean!" The Head tapped the table irritably. "What about Aberforss? He was already a problem even before this little rebellion started: clearly a dissident, but we can scarcely exile him to Esilia where he can make even more trouble. I'll order his secure facility to release him to your experimental team. If this drug suite tames Aberforss, I'll be impressed."

CHAPTER FOURTEEN

Yanni felt sure the Thing by the river wasn't ghosts or sprites or ifreets. And even if it was, they were only disembodied spirits that a real man wouldn't be afraid of. Now it was a matter of his personal honor to go back there.

The boy hadn't been supposed to get so close to the army's line of march, but when had that ever stopped a boy from spying on soldiers? He'd spent the greater part of a day lying along a rock ledge, watching the entertaining confusion of the supply train, before his aunt heard him retailing the details to a clump of envious younger kids. She clouted him on the spot, and the next day dragged him by the ear to the village school. "And if you play truant again, it won't be me, but your uncle Ektor you'll be explaining yourself to!"

Uncle Ektor had a heavy hand, and considered it part of his duty to his dead brother to thrash Yanni periodically on the grounds that he had undoubtedly done something to deserve it. Yanni sulked and brooded for an entire two days before the Night of the Screams.

Most of the villagers claimed that they hadn't heard a thing, they were far too tired after the day's work to sit up late imagining things. But while they asserted this, they looked over their shoulders. The men clicked worry beads and the wives broke off pieces of the morning flatbread to lay on the black stone sacred to the old gods of the mountain, the ones who'd been displaced when deportees left the arid plains to build up into the hills.

The children were more forthright, if no more truthful. No boy in the village would admit to having slept through the previous night. "Ghosts," one of them boasted. "My cousin's wife's father walked for three nights after he died and he made noises just like that!"

"Huh," said another one. "There's no such thing as ghosts. It was the White Woman, warning us that someone's going to die."

"*All night?* Don't be stupid. It was ifreets."

"No ifreets in the mountains…"

"There are now. They prob'ly followed the army up from the flat-lands." The speaker saw Yanni's lips twitch. "Don't believe in ifreets, Yanni? What do *you* reckon it was, then, squealing and shrieking half the night in a dozen voices?"

"I think…" That right there was where it became a matter of honor, when Yanni's mouth outraced his brain. "*I* think I'm going back to the river road after school, to try and find out what really made those noises." *No! No! This is a very bad idea*, his brain gibbered – too late.

"Why put it off?"

Yanni's shoulders twitched. "Why invite Uncle Ektor to belt me again for skipping school? He does it often enough as it is."

That saved his honor for the time being, as two of the speculating boys were his cousins and agreed that a belting from Ektor was nothing to incur lightly.

But then he had all day in school to think about it.

"Don't get caught out there after dark," one of his cousins warned him when he started off for the river.

"Why not? I'm not afraid of the dark, are you? Oh, I forgot. You believe in ghosts and the White Woman. You probably are afraid."

But Yanni's steps were dragging as he made his way through the needle trees to the ledge where he'd built a screen of dead branches to hide him while he watched the soldiers. The closer he got, the worse he felt about it. Something smelled bad... And the fat, heavy blackflies were buzzing. He slapped one away from his face. Too bad it had stopped raining; they never came out when it was wet. One good thing about rain...

His screen of branches looked pathetically bare; all the needles had fallen off the dead limbs. But maybe he wouldn't need it. He didn't hear anybody moving on the river road; he didn't hear anything but the buzzing of the blackflies. Probably the supply train had finally gotten themselves organized and marched on into the high mountains. He would just take a look, then he could go back and tell his scaredy-cat cousins that there was nothing on the river road and certainly no sign of anything supernatural.

Except... there was *something*. Not soldiers in their smartcloth grey and green uniforms that blended in with the rocks and trees; some red things, each standing next to a tree, each the height of a man, and he did *not* believe in ifreets. Even if there were pale strips of something flapping in the trees overhead. Paper, he told himself. Or rags. *Not* ifreet wings.

Yanni clenched his teeth and walked to the far edge of the tree line, some twenty feet beyond his screened ledge, where he could see exactly what the red things were.

Then he vomited on the carpet of needles for quite a long time, until he thought he could feel his empty stomach flapping against his backbone, and he wanted to rinse the sour taste out of his mouth but going to the river would mean going past... more of those...

He ran back to the village, stuck his head under the spring that fell into a rock-walled basin and frantically gulped cold water, but it wanted to come right up again.

"Boy! What are you doing, fouling our water? Get your scabby head out of there before I thrash you!"

There was something almost comforting in the familiar threat; being beaten, however unpleasant, was part of ordinary life.

And Uncle Ektor was not at all a bad person to grasp at when you were on the verge of disgracing yourself by shivering and crying. His uncle's broad shoulder sheltered him until Yanni was able to stop gulping and tell what he'd found by the river.

"They were men. I think. Harmonicas – soldiers – I think, but they weren't wearing their uniforms any more. They were all red, and somebody had hung strips of their skin in the branches, and, and their *eyes*, and...."

"Look at me, boy."

At the sight of his uncle's face, taut and rigid with anger, Yanni thought that he was perhaps about to get the worst beating of his life.

"You're not making this up, are you?"

Yanni shook his head. "I swear it's true. I... I swear by the black stone. It must have been the Old Gods, *people* wouldn't do all that to people, they're angry because we came into their country..."

Ektor shook him by the shoulders. "Stop babbling hysterical nonsense. It was my father's grandfather built the first house here, I don't think the Old Gods waited five generations and then avenged themselves on the wrong people. I suppose I'd better go and see for myself. You go home, and tell your aunt I said to give you some flatbread and cheese to replace the stuff you vomited up. Good sharp new cheese will take the taste out of your mouth."

In the end it was half the village men who went down to the river. Ektor had wanted to borrow the only holorecorder in the village, which was the schoolteacher's treasure and delight. He wouldn't lend out the recorder unless he got to come too, and the teacher's brother went with the teacher, and so on until there was a virtual parade of scowling, black-mustachioed men marching towards the river valley. But Uncle Ektor went first.

They sent two men back for shovels, and after that nobody returned until well after dark.

Lying awake in the niche where he slept, just an extension of the outer wall really, Yanni heard his uncle talking to Aunt Meli. "Never seen anything like it… I hate the Harmonicas as much as anyone, but that wasn't war; it was torture. Looks like Mavros Karamanlis' work, remember that farmer in Davlis who wouldn't contribute to his gang? Like that, but worse. This time there was a lot of… detailed work. Small knife. Done before they died, from all the blood."

"*Panayamu.*" There was a rustle of fabric; Aunt Meli crossing herself three times. "So, he's learned more evil."

Ektor sighed. "I'd heard that Angelos Angelu had joined up with him. Calls himself Angelos Thanatu now. He likes to use this little curved knife, you know?"

"Well, what are you going to do about it?" Meli's voice was sharp.

"What can I do? They're fighting the Harmonicas. You want to give in to the Harmonicas, be slaves to Harmony, see our boys raised as slaves?"

"Better slaves than damned to eternity. Have you thought about what happens if we owe our independence to those like Mavros? He needs to be stopped *now*, before we fall from rebellion into civil war."

Ektor gave another heavy sigh. "You always could think and talk rings around me, Meli. But *I* can't put Mavros Karamanlis out of business. And those who maybe could, are busy fighting Harmonicas themselves."

"Then send the holos to someone who can do it." Meli paused. "Send them to the so-called governor. Stinking Billy's almost as vicious as Mavros; he should be able to deal with them."

"Hmm." Ektor scratched his chin. "No, I can't communicate with Stinking Billy. That would be treason. But if I go visit your cousin Demitris… His place is practically out on the plains. Good communications with the capital. Encode the holos, send them in one short burst. Not to the governor. To the newser offices. If they all have the material, they'll be falling over themselves to be the ones who get it out first. Then the Harmonicas will be forced to take notice."

It all sounded needlessly complicated to Yanni. But at least Uncle Ektor seemed to have everything under control.

* * *

"We need a victory," Andrus told General Dayvson. They were riding two relatively compliant donkeys that plodded up the track beside the river at a pace that allowed ample time for conversation. "No, let me rephrase that. *You* need a victory – something to show the common people why we're fighting this war – if you want to keep your position."

"You think I'm that desperate to keep command? I will happily hand over the army to whatever poor fool the Committee taps next. Just as soon as I have Isovel back."

"Then you need to buy the time to search for her. No, listen! I know you despise me and everyone in the Bureau for Concord. Sometimes I despise this job myself. But I *do* know politics. You don't do politics; I respect that. But with even more respect, General, you may not be interested in politics but politics is interested in you."

"Therefore, your advice that I should win?" Rauf Dayvson snorted. "You know, I had actually been thinking along those lines myself."

"My advice," Andrus said stiffly, "is that you should pay heed to the political issues back home. This morning, when we crossed that ridge line, I was able to establish direct communication with headquarters for a short time. They passed on to me the latest news from Harmony."

"So?"

"General, it's bad. Very bad. Those stragglers who never caught up with the supply train after it resumed marching? They were tortured to death by guerrillas and left for the locals to find. Newsers got wind of it somehow, and got *pictures* which they've been broadcasting all over Harmony."

"Discord. Dissonance. Sour notes! Are you telling me *Harmony City* knows what's happened to my troops before I do?" Dayvson chewed on his short gray mustache. "*I* should have known about this. Who kept it from me?" He glared at Andrus.

"Communications are much better in the plains. And... um... there wasn't a rider..."

"I sent Lieutenant Kenzi back to form up the last of the supply train. He should have..." Dayvson's voice trailed off. "Was he killed too?"

"Probably." Andrus swallowed. "It's... hard to tell. I captured some stills from the holos on my wristcom. I can show you..."

"Tonight. My tent. This isn't something to be discussed in the middle of the day's march." Dayvson dismissed Andrus with a sharp nod and urged his donkey forward to catch up with the staff officers at the head of the column.

The stills were bad enough; the messages from CenCom were worse. "What do they mean," Dayvson exploded that night, "I'm instructed to withdraw my forces to the plains? Do they have *any idea* what it's cost us to get them this far into the mountains?"

The costs were less than they had been, as each guerrilla attack and each loss made Dayvson aware of his oversights. The column marched in close order now, with scouts in the woods on each flank and taking point. The scouts were sent out in pairs, to discourage any individual from taking the chance to desert. And from tonight, the remnants of the baggage train would march with the main column at all times. There would be an armed rear guard to protect them, and riders to warn him if they began to straggle. He felt that he was finally figuring out how to run this war. *Too late for Kenzi*. But that thought made him even more determined to push on.

Andrus sighed. "I think the Committee are more concerned with what it may cost them to keep going. The marches in Harmony City are turning into riots. Our losses have been bad enough that we need to draft replacement soldiers."

"So? There hasn't been any trouble with the draft."

"Not yet. But we ran out of slum dregs to draft some time ago. Each man we take now has a family – parents, maybe a wife and children – that resents our taking him. Has a job that goes unfilled without him, and that kicks the economy down even more. And now that these holos have been spread…"

Dayvson expressed himself pithily, if blasphemously, on the subject of a Central Committee that couldn't even keep the newsers on a leash.

"Agreed," said Andrus, "but they can't exactly deport them, can they?"

"Draft'em," Dayvson snarled.

"Not practical. All the newsers have connections in the Central Committee or high up in some Bureau or other. And in any case, it's too late. *Nobody* is going to comply with a draft that sends them out to a rebel continent where they're tortured and killed. Central needs you to get out of the mountains before there's an outright revolt in the city. They're afraid. They sent all their peace officers off with the army and now they haven't the power to put down a riot. Once the mob finds that out...." Andrus shook his head.

"Let them quiver. They're not out here where there's something real to be afraid of. Tell them to find a pointy stake and sit on it, I'll come back after I've found and destroyed these nests of traitors."

"Yes, well… First find your traitors, eh? There's a lot of territory to search, and these rebels know the land; we don't. Their small groups can move fast; our column is tied to the speed of the slowest marchers. They can blend in with the locals; we stand out."

"Doesn't help, Andrus, to have you listing the problems. We can and *will* beat these raggedy amateurs. And – you know I'm not going to retreat without Isovel."

Andrus bowed and eased out of the general's tent, thinking furiously. This obsession with his daughter was going to ruin Dayvson. And it might ruin him too, as the political officer who couldn't rein in his subject. Outright defiance of the Committee? Dayvson would be recalled in disgrace – most likely, so would Andrus – while somebody more pliable took over the army.

Which would, Andrus realized, mean more losses, more deaths, more soldiers vulnerable to these vicious traitors. Because Dayvson was the only remotely competent senior officer in Harmony's hastily assembled army.

"What a war!" he thought. "The commanding officer reads history books to figure out how to lead an invading army. And the rebels are probably reading books on how to conduct an asymmetric war. We should all drop this nonsense and get back to things we know how to do."

It was at that moment that he was visited by the blinding light of inspiration. He could save Dayvson. He could save his own career.

And he might just be able to save Harmony while he was at it.

CHAPTER FIFTEEN

Renzi had been busy with the printer in the back of the library tent all morning, while Isovel sat at his table and read. This Reference Library the rebels set such store by was strange and hypnotically interesting. Some of the books contained such free-wheeling debates on dangerous ideas that she got confused and often felt that neither side was right and they were both insane. "States" were like Districts, she decided, but why debate over how much independent power they should have? The Districts simply implemented the Central Committee's plans; how else could society have uniform harmony? Then they worried about whether a strong central government would protect or diminish individual liberty, as though liberty was a good in itself rather than a means for individuals to come to harmony. And then…

Isovel kept swearing that she wouldn't go on looking at these risky, tricky books that seemed designed to destroy all her principles. But the ideas kept nagging at her mind, and every day she gave in again to the temptation to read what she would never, ever have a chance to read at home. Because it was perfectly clear why these books had been removed from Harmony's collection; they were full of seditious ideas that would only whip up the mob and encourage them in discord. It would be a serious mistake to let just anybody read them.

She, however, was an educated person who collected and annotated references for the historical papers her father used to write when he was just a professor. She had the mental stability and the critical thinking to see through false arguments.

And puzzling out the meaning of these documents through their archaic language and spelling helped her not to think about people she would never see again and who were really of no significance at all in her real life. Back on Harmony. Where nobody ever argued. And that was better, wasn't it? And didn't she long to return to the comforts and peace of home?

Of course she did.

She just – well – wasn't in any hurry to leave, that was all.

The tent was beginning to smell of the ink Renzi fed the printer. She wondered if he would help her move the table outside, so that she could read in the fresh air. But when she went back to ask, he was totally occupied in coaxing his printed sheets through the outdated printer which seemed to want to mangle each page as it passed between the rollers. Isovel shook her head at the elaborate insults he was heaping on the printer, which was apparently the offspring of a diseased donkey and a rabid greatcat.

Who even used 2-D printers any more, when for the same price you could get an all-in-one that would actually fab small items in its 3-D mode? she asked Renzi. This device couldn't do anything useful like that.

He looked up and wiped the sweat out of his eyes with the back of one hand, in the process smearing the blotch of ink that he'd somehow gotten on one temple.

"Depends how you define *useful.* I've told you, ideas are our best weapons." He thumped the small pile of finished sheets with one hand. "These will do far more than blasters to discourage the damned Harmonicas, oh sorry, your compatriots I mean."

"Indeed!" Isovel extracted a sheet from the pile and wandered outside to read it in natural light, with a supercilious smile as she skimmed the bold printing. Renzi was delusional if he thought that this obvious pack of lies would have any effect on people like her father. Harmony forces defeated here, here, and here? The invading column losing men daily? All lies…

But would the grunts know that? And the last paragraph was downright scary. It urged the common soldiers to desert now rather than "marching through a hostile land to be picked off one by one, leaving your bones to crumble away in a foreign country for the sake of politicians who never did you any good." Melodramatic language – but then, it was aimed at people who spent their free hours drinking and watching cheap holodramas. And the next sentences were genuinely worrisome, offering deserters a warm welcome, good food, and a section of Esilian land after the war.

Isobel's brows were drawn together, two sharp vertical lines cut into her forehead, by the time she finished reading. Of course it was all lies and false promises; for one thing, only the governor had authority to approve land grants. But at home, one understood that the populace lacked critical thinking skills, and it would have been a crime to confuse them with stuff like this. Would this really affect the grunts?

She remembered the chip on Jonny Kelso's shoulder. Yes. Some of them were primed and ready for any rabble-rousing rhetoric that pretended to offer them a better deal in life. These leaflets might be only a small irritation, but her father and his staff officers really had enough to worry about without having sedition preached through the ranks.

She folded the offending sheet twice and tucked it into her sleeve, then went back in to see what she could do.

The grating noises had stopped; so had Renzi's inventive stream of insults. He was sitting on a camp stool, leaning his head back against the printer.

"Done?"

"Oh, hell, no. The colonel wants five times this many flyers by tonight; he's going to distribute them to every band on the mountain, so they can seed the entire length of the column with them. We got a great response with the first flyer. I'm just tired and frustrated with nursing this aborted obscenity of a machine. We can't afford to have every third flyer crumpled or smeared; I don't have enough ink to waste it."

"Will people be coming to here to pick them up?" *Gabrel.* Not that it mattered to her in the slightest. But, *Gabrel,* her heart insisted.

"Yup. That's why I gotta finish the job today. Otherwise we'll have every guerrilla captain and lieutenant on the mountain complaining about kicking their heels waiting for stupid *paperwork.* And their men without leaders."

"You'd think they would send an errand boy instead of coming themselves."

"Well, a few might have that much sense," Renzi allowed. "But too damned many of them are glory hounds. They won't delegate anything and they always want to get the latest gossip directly from the base."

"And now the printer's breaking down," Isovel said sympathetically. "What a disaster for you!"

Renzi's half-closed eyes shot open. "It's *not* breaking down. It's *always* been cranky like this." But he looked alarmed. Good.

"Indeed? Funny, I took a course in tech repair, and your printer sounds *exactly* like one of the overstressed machines we had to refurbish. If the operators had only brought them to us earlier we could have recalibrated them so that they wouldn't be stressed to destruction."

"You took tech repair?"

Isovel shrugged. "Only two semesters. I can't work with heavy equipment, just minor appliances like printers and chronos." She waited, hardly breathing, to see if Renzi would take the bait.

"You can fix *printers*? Oh, my. We don't have anybody who knows his way around these new machines."

Isovel decided it would be tactless to mention that on Harmony, nobody would call an obsolete 2D printer a "new" machine.

"Could you – would you –" Renzi swallowed whatever he was going to say next. "No, it's not fair to ask you to look at the spavined mule of a machine. I keep forgetting that you're on the other side."

"So do I." Isovel switched on her Grade Three smile, the one that had distracted more than half of the colonel's young officers. "But I'm bored, and I'd like to make some repayment for your generous hospitality. So why don't you take your headache over to the mess tent and treat it with a cup of kahve, while I look over your printer and see if there's anything I can do?"

The idiot actually fell for that. I can't believe he was Gabrel's best friend growing up… oh well, he's not stupid. Just insufficiently paranoid.

Alone in the library tent, Isovel pushed up her sleeves, swung the camp stool around to face the back of the printer, and set out to see just what she could do. Hmm, the snap-in solar cells snapped out easily enough. She might be able to degrade the shiny contacts enough to spoil the power supply, but it would be more satisfying and wreak more havoc if she got inside and messed with the wiring… Ha! Here was a black panel covered with warnings from "Disable power before removing this panel," to "Don't immerse this machine in water."

Isovel always wondered about those general-purpose warnings. Did anyone really have to be told not to put their home printer in the bathtub? Never mind, the first warning told her all she needed to know: the panel could be removed. And a look at the accompanying picture showed two pairs of tabs, one on each top corner of the panel, being pinched together. The tabs were stiff enough to hurt her fingers, but finally gave way and allowed her to fold the panel down along its hinged bottom edge. Success! Now she was looking at a tangle of wires running from the power points to the interior of the printer.

If she really had the tech training she'd implied, she might be able to do something subtle, like switching just enough wires to make the machine misinterpret every command. Oh, well, at least she knew enough to wreak her own kind of havoc.

Renzi kept a utility knife in his top drawer. *Nice and sharp. Sturdy, too.* Isovel used the knife to worry individual wires completely free, tucking them into her sleeve as she collected them. These *people don't do machinery; I bet they'll have to send to the plains for more insulated wire.* She used the sharp edge of the knife to strip the insulation from randomly selected samples of the remaining wires. *What else? Ah, the feed thickness sensors. Destroy, or just disable?* If she disconnected them but left the sensors in place, it would take them a while to figure out why the machine had become a paper-shredding monster. That was assuming they could recover to the point of making it run again, of course… She snapped the panel back in, replaced the solar cells and occupied herself until Renzi got back by tearing up the existing flyers and hiding the shreds.

"Where are the flyers?" Renzi asked the minute he came back to the printing area.

Stuffing the chair cushions. "Oh, some guy came for them."

"Which group?"

Isovel shrugged. "He didn't say. And I was busy working on your printer." Would it be wise to leave now, before Renzi found out what she'd been up to? Oh, well. It wasn't like she could pretend innocence. And she did want to see if her improvised sabotage had worked.

"It doesn't matter which group, Renzi. Whoever doesn't show up tonight will be the one who collected his supply early." That was Colonel Travis. Oh, dissonance! Renzi might lose his temper when the printer failed, but the colonel could have her executed. Except he wouldn't do that. To a valuable hostage. She hoped.

"Well, I'd better get started again. I want to have some flyers in hand for the next early bird." He glanced at Isovel. "Were you able to do anything with The Monster?"

"I hope so," Isovel said.

"Guess we'll just have to see how she goes." Isovel moved out of the way so that Renzi could snap the solar power cells back in place. He checked ink and liquid flimsy levels and then flipped the switch that should start the printer generating a new flimsy with the programmed text inked onto the surface.

Sparks shot out of the back of the printer and Renzi hastily flipped the switch off again. "What was *that?*"

"Um, temporary power surge following an unscheduled disconnection," Isovel improvised. "Sometimes these older units aren't properly shielded, so you might want to stand back for a few minutes after you power on." And with any luck, a few minutes of electricity pouring through crossed wires without insulation should weld some of those wires together and create solid disaster zones that nobody could disentangle.

Renzi looked dubious but followed Isovel's suggestion, flipping the switch at arm's length and quickly backing up a couple of steps. He and the colonel and she were all pressed against the bookshelf now.

And The Monster performed. Isovel started to grin. There were sparks and snaps, arcs of light, black smoke… It was glorious!

Colonel Travis held Renzi's arm when he started forward to turn the printer off again. "Best not touch it." He glanced around the library tent, removed a lightweight wooden stay from the roof structure. Held it out, tried to use it to flip the switch, didn't have the leverage. Snapped the stick down along the side of the printer with enough force to both flip the switch and break the printer.

"What *did you do to my printer?*" For the first time, Isovel saw the capacity for violence in Renzi. He reached out towards her, only to be intercepted by the colonel.

"Renzi. We don't beat prisoners. And we don't hit *girls*. No matter how sly and sneaking and vicious they turn out to be." He glared at Isovel.

She lifted her chin. "You forget, Colonel. We are not on the same side. It's my duty to hamper your plans in any way possible."

"Try not to make me forget that part about not hitting girls," the colonel said tersely. "It wasn't enough for you to distract half of my officers, you had to move up to sabotage? More fool me, for thinking that we could all act like civilized beings here!"

"That was an impressive way to repay our hospitality," Renzi chimed in.

The colonel glanced at him. "So that was how she conned you into leaving her alone with the printer? Idiot. I'll deal with you later." He blew a whistle and two very young men edged past the tent flap. "Forget escorting me," Colonel Travis said. "Escort *her*. Straight to the hospital tent. She's not to leave it and nobody is to talk to her. She's a very dangerous prisoner." As the young men took charge of Isovel, he muttered under his breath, "And a damned nuisance!"

CHAPTER SIXTEEN

Andrus looked around the rebel base and wondered why they felt the need to guard it with multiple sentries and passwords. There was nothing here but tents and rocks, muddy black paths and rain-sodden pale grass. It was all but incomprehensible that this rag-tag bunch of volunteers, lacking even uniforms, had been able to inflict such losses on the Harmony Expeditionary Force. He supposed it helped that the rebels were used to poverty and backwardness. This so-called "colonel" didn't have to coddle his guerrillas the way Harmony had to take care of the city-bred scum they were trying to transform into soldiers. And the rebels probably didn't value human life the way a civilized country did.

A sharp breeze swept across the little plateau in the center of the base, and Andrus was grateful for the smartcloth uniform that kept him warm and dry. How did the ragged "soldiers" like the ones who'd brought him in manage when a cold wind followed the rain that soaked their clothing? Oh well, they were used to it; they wouldn't feel these things the way civilized people did.

"How much longer will "Colonel" Travis be?" he asked the yokel who'd been assigned to guard him.

The rebel shrugged, reached under his shirt to scratch vigorously, and yawned.

"I asked you a question, man!" Altogether deplorable. These troops had no concept of discipline.

The rebel looked down at him. "You're worried about being late for your next appointment, maybe?"

Andrus began to regret having taken the chair he was offered. It was hard to impress these bumpkins with his superiority when they could all look down on him. But his feet hurt. If he'd realized just how much walking, scrambling, and climbing lay between the Expeditionary Force and the rebels' base, he'd never have set off in the pre-dawn darkness with his little white flag, hoping to be challenged by somebody who would take him to the base.

The "colonel", when he was finally available, didn't come to meet Andrus, but had him escorted to a small tent that was marginally less shabby than the ones on either side.

"Please, sit," said the unimpressive rebel leader.

Andrus took the offered camp stool and sat quietly, wondering how much he should simplify his terms to communicate with this tired middle-aged man who looked totally overwhelmed by the responsibility that had been thrust upon him. At least Rauf Dayvson, stubborn though he might be, wore his uniform with style and looked the part of a gallant military leader. This "Colonel" Travis looked like an aging schoolteacher – the kind who was always teased unmercifully by the bad boys.

"Well? I assume you went to this effort because you had something to say," Travis snapped.

Andrus blinked and scrambled to retrieve his thoughts. "I've come to end a stalemate that does neither of us any good. My principals –"

"General Dayvson?"

Andrus straightened his tired shoulders. "I have the good fortune to report to a much higher level than the good General!"

"Ah – your Central Committee, I assume?"

"Yes."

"Divided command," the colonel mused. "How's that working out for you Harmonicas?"

"It wouldn't be a problem if –" Andrus stopped himself. "There are occasional impasses," he said. "We appear to have one right now. You don't want our army here. The Central Committee is willing to agree to a temporary withdrawal of forces pending a more lasting treaty."

"Good. Go do it, then we'll talk."

"But I fear that General Dayvson's respect for the Committee is overridden by concern for his daughter. If I could bring her back I feel sure the General would abide by any decision you and I agreed on."

"You want her back." The colonel seemed bemused. "You *want* her back. *You* want *her* back?" He might have been trying different inflections on a string of nonsense syllables, searching for meaning.

"In good condition," Andrus appended. Who knew what this rabble had done to the girl? "If she's… damaged… in any obvious way… her death, properly witnessed, would be an alternative solution." Not a good one, but better than bringing back a shattered torture victim whose condition would only inflame the general.

The colonel whistled – very undignified for a man in his position, but doubtless the native knew no better. "I'd heard you people were cold, but not that you were willing to kill your own for political gain!"

"I did not say that was my object," Andrus pointed out. "I would much prefer returning her to her father in good condition. That would make it much easier to persuade him to honor the wishes of the Committee."

"Oh, *she's* all right," said the colonel, with an odd emphasis suggesting that some other things – men? equipment? – were not in as good shape. "And you can have her back with my blessing. Mirez! I want a guard and a guide to escort this gentleman and Citizen Dayvson back to the Harmony army."

Andrus blinked again. He had hardly expected to achieve his goal quite so easily. What was the catch here?"

He watched and listened carefully as Mirez and the colonel discussed – quite openly, right in front of him – how many men would be required to guarantee the hostage's safe return.

"Two men should be enough," said Lieutenant Mirez.

"You'll settle for that?"

"Oh. *I'm* in charge of this effort? Then I want six men. At a minimum."

"Of course you're in charge. You're the only officer I'm sure hasn't fallen for her."

Mirez smiled slightly. "I don't think she's ever figured out that Gabrel's more my type."

With a little haggling the colonel beat him down to three armed guards and a guide. It was all quite undignified and unsuitable, but these people seemed to have no concept of proper behavior.

"I'd have liked to entertain you tonight," the colonel said. "We could have had a civilized chat about this unfortunate war; you seem like a man who can rise above petty considerations of pride and revenge. But I quite understand your desire to reunite Miss Dayvson with her father as soon as possible. If you leave at once, you should be able to rejoin the column before dark."

Andrus didn't recall having expressed such a desire, and he was tired and footsore from the journey here. And how did Travis know exactly where the column was? Never mind; he'd achieved his aim with amazing ease, now it would be as well to get away with the girl before the colonel had second thoughts.

* * *

"We're actually not that far from the head of the column," Andrus assured Isovel. "You'll be reunited with your father well before dark."

"Thank you," Isovel said through stiff lips.

She felt as though his voice were coming to her from an immeasurable distance; from the other side of an invisible wall that separated her from reality. A wall she'd been building around herself ever since Colonel Travis had hustled her out of camp. Reality hurt; in reality she was to have no chance even to say good-bye to Gabrel. In reality he had dropped her like a hot potato as soon as he decently could after she'd caused him to kill Jesse, and had avoided the base camp ever since because he couldn't stand even to see her. In reality she was the enemy. Hadn't she been doing her best to sabotage the rebel operations?

Reality was vastly overrated.

All the while she'd been at the base – not that long, really – she'd clung, without knowing it, to a tiny, infinitesimal scrap of hope. Gabrel *might* report to Colonel Travis in person. He *might* not hate her for her part in Jesse's death.

It was only now, when she'd lost it, that she realized how much comfort that last hope had been. She couldn't exactly fantasize that a captain of irregular forces would drop in to visit the enemy army. And if what Andrus said of the Central Committee was true, the Expeditionary Force would soon be withdrawing to the plains, even farther from…

From nobody she expected to see again. Anyway, he'd lied to her. That stupid affair with Jonny made her feel like a cradle-robber; it was farcical to have repeated the mistake with an enemy soldier, of all people! Really, it was for the best that she was going back to her own people.

Isovel blinked away tears and concentrated fiercely on her surroundings. The donkey she rode had been picking its way down the mountain without her guidance. Now she looked around her and tried to memorize everything around her. They were passing through a sort of clearing – well, a place where the rocky bones of the mountain surfaced and discouraged most trees. Pale, rain-sodden tall grasses flopped over every patch of dirt, every crack in the naked boulders. Behind them was the dark forest of needle trees; ahead, more forest, but with a sprinkling of gold-maples that lightened the gloom under the needle trees. The air was crisp, no longer soggy with unshed rain; the sky was a distant, brilliant blue against which the rare branches of gold-maple flew golden and scarlet flags. *I will remember this. And I will remember that it was beautiful.*

A sound from the trail ahead startled her. Someone coming towards them? Who cared? She prepared to scowl at whoever had interrupted her reverie.

"Gabrel! What are you doing here?" Lieutenant Mirez exclaimed as the approaching figure came out of the shadows.

"That's *Captain* Gabrel to you, infant. And I might ask you the same question." He glanced at Isovel and Andrus. "Has peace been declared, and nobody told me?"

"Steps towards a peace, maybe. We give the girl back, and the army withdraws from the mountains."

Gabrel's dark brows drew together. "What's the good of that? We need to keep the army tied up in the mountains, where we can raid and harass them and break their nerve."

"Look," Mirez said, "I know you've been having fun and finding new ways to make the Harmonica soldiers' lives interesting, but you can't expect Colonel Travis to conduct policy solely on the basis of what amuses his youngest captain. If you want to argue, go talk to the colonel."

Gabrel looked at Isovel but continued talking to Mirez. "That's where I'm headed. Got word he wants to see me. About this?"

Mirez shrugged. "I wouldn't know. I, as you've pointed out, am merely a lowly lieutenant."

"But a very trusted one," said Gabrel, "to be charged with escorting such a valuable package. I'm acquainted with the lady; who's her friend?"

"A political." Mirez might have said, "A maggot," in the same tone.

"Sent to negotiate?"

"Something like that. Look, Captain, this discussion is above my pay grade and I need to get on, or we'll be climbing back by moonlight."

"You can wait another five minutes," Gabrel told him. "I have a little unfinished business to settle with the lady."

"Concerning?"

"Above your pay grade," Gabrel snapped.

"Fine. Go ahead."

Gabrel glared at him. "You'll allow us a little privacy." It wasn't a request.

Mirez bowed ironically. "Take her aside if you like. But stay within sight. I do have a responsibility here; I'm sworn to return her undamaged."

"I wasn't planning to damage her." Gabrel stepped past Mirez and offered Isovel his hand to dismount.

Touching him – was a mistake. Possibly for both of them; Isovel fought to keep her composure, while Gabrel inhaled sharply and removed his hand as soon as she was on her feet. He bowed slightly and waved towards the patch of bare rock Mirez had indicated. "After you."

The imaginary wall melted; all her walls collapsed. Her hands shook as she walked away from the escort group. Did Gabrel know that she had no defenses against him? Did he care?

When they were well out of earshot of the others, she stopped and turned to him. She'd meant to raise one eyebrow, to be the epitome of cool self-possession. But that possibility had melted away when she touched his hand.

He looked ill. She was willing to bet the idiot had been abusing his bad knee again, once she and Jesse weren't around to nag him about it… *Jesse.*

"I – didn't know you were leaving us so soon. I'd been meaning to ask you…" His voice trailed off into a bare thread.

"Ask me?" Discord! She still couldn't raise an eyebrow. She could only wait, defenseless, for whatever he might want to say.

"I hadn't meant to bring this up so soon. I thought I – we – had time. But if you're going away now… Had you ever considered…" He gestured around them, a wave of his hand taking in the crisp blue air and the flags of gold-maple. "This part of Esilia is beautiful, isn't it? I mean, you know now that it's not all hot, dusty plains… Do you think… Is there any possibility that you might consider staying here? In Esilia. I mean. After the war – well, of course not, I'm an idiot, forget I said anything, I know you hate it here…"

"I don't hate it here." Isvel couldn't get any more past her dry throat. Where Gabrel was babbling, she was trapped in silence.

"Oh, really?" His face brightened. "Then... do you think you could get used to it? I – I mean... to *me*, really."

I already am. Your face will follow me in dreams for the rest of my life. Isovel clamped down the traitorous urge to go all sentimental and squishy.

"I – have to return to the army. It's part of the deal."

The life went out of Gabrel's face. "I see. And I, of course, have to report to my superior officer. It would seem that, for the moment, our paths lie in opposite directions."

"So it would seem."

"I have only one argument left." But instead of voicing it, Gabrel turned around and shouted, "Mirez!"

"Sir?"

"A little privacy, if you please...Turn your back, idiot! And that goes for the rest of you as well!"

They were of a height; his lips met hers, his hands were hard and forceful on her back, crushing her against him. Isovel's head swam and she melted against him.

She was still intoxicated when he stepped back. "All right, then. Go back – for now – if you insist," he told her. "I know better than to fight your insane sense of duty. But don't get too settled. I *will* come for you."

CHAPTER SEVENTEEN

The library tent was large enough to accommodate Renzi, a bookcase, a table and chairs, and a curtained-off space at the back that used to be reserved for printing. Back when he'd had a printer, that was.

It was not anywhere near large enough to contain his friend's nervous energy. Sitting across from Renzi, Gabrel constantly shifted his weight, drummed his fingers on the table top, cracked his knuckles, and tilted his chair back at an angle just five degrees away from disaster.

So much for a nice afternoon reconnecting with his oldest friend.

"Oh, go ahead and pace," Renzi snapped the third time Gabrel tilted his chair to the point of eliciting creaks of protest from the abused frame. "You're driving me crazy."

Gabrel sat forward, elbows on the table, and started cracking his knuckles. Again. "There's not enough room to pace properly in here. I need more than three strides at a time to get my brain working."

"Then go outside and get it over with."

"Not enough privacy. I need to talk to you. New orders – I'm not sure what to do. Thought I could bounce ideas off of you."

Renzi snorted. "Instead of bouncing yourself off the tent walls? Let's go for a walk. At least you can burn off some of that energy."

The crisp fall air, scented with resin from the needle trees, seemed to give Gabrel even more energy. He set a pace that Renzi could barely match, and even that much speed precluded using his breath for anything as trivial as conversation. *Too much time sitting in the tent because I'm ashamed to face my brother officers. I should use the exercise ground every day.*

There was a solitary runner on the circular track to which Colonel Travis had sacrificed the largest patch of sort-of level ground inside the lines of the base. Gabrel turned onto the track, hands clasped behind him, and glowered at the jogging private. Renzi was not surprised that the runner suddenly discovered that he'd exercised enough; Gabrel in one of his moods exuded a nearly-visible force field twanging with tension.

At least the track was flat. Mostly. Renzi slowed to a reasonable walking pace and waited for Gabrel to notice.

A hundred steps later, when his figure had almost blended with the darkening sky, Gabrel glanced to his right and abruptly stopped walking, waiting for Renzi to catch up. "Running you off your feet? Sorry!"

"I haven't been scrambling up and down mountains like you," Renzi said. *Because I'm a useless coward who can't take combat duty.*

Gabrel glanced at him. "Colonel Travis doesn't think you're useless. Or a coward. Neither do I."

"Damn it, Gabrel. I hate that magical mind-reading thing you do."

"Nothing magical about it. I can't do it with anybody except—" Gabrel paused and restarted the sentence. "I can't do it with most people. It's just that I've known you so long. And your body language is – well, don't ever play poker, okay, Renzi?"

"Ha! What about *your* body language? Here you are fizzing with energy to the point you can't sit still. You're practically shouting, "New orders! New action!""

The track curved to the left; the dense forest of needle trees to their right blocked the setting sun.

"See? You can do it too. Only you got it partly wrong. My body language is shouting, 'New orders! Help!'"

"Well, I'm the last person you should come to for help in a fight. I thought everybody knew that by now."

"Get the damned chip off your shoulder. You'd be surprised how many people respect and honor your decision. Those of us who send men to die, who kill for an idea… Some of us think you're our last hope of remaining human."

"Some decision!" Gabrel wouldn't respect him if he knew the truth, if he'd seen the shivering, shaking *thing* wearing Renzi's face after Dun Valley.

"Well… cowards refuse to go into danger. *You* told the colonel that you wouldn't order any more men to die. That may disqualify you as an active-duty officer, but there are other ways to serve and you've found one. Now, enough about you!" Gabrel's grin flashed white in the gathering darkness. "I hauled you out here to talk about *my* problems!"

Renzi spread his hands out. "So talk."

The silence stretched between them, broken only by the scuffing of their boots on the hard-packed earth of the track. Just when Renzi had stopped expecting a response, he heard the quick inhalation that meant Gabrel was preparing to say something difficult.

"Colonel Travis wants me to take out Mavros Karamanlis and his gang."

"With – what have you got, twelve men? You and what army?"

"Oh, he's giving me all the resources he can. Now that we're officially negotiating with the army, we don't need people picking them off and trying to ruin morale. He says. Lorens and Sandoval are instructed to report to me for this exercise."

"That's all?" Lieutenant Lorens had five men; Sandoval, eight.

"Everybody else is either significantly older than I am or outranks me." Gabrel gritted his teeth. "I *hate* being the Young Officer."

"Wait a while," Renzi said, "that problem will cure itself."

"But not before this action."

"No… Does this have anything to do with the pictures that Harmonica spy showed the colonel?"

"He called himself a political officer, not a spy… I wonder why the colonel even bothers with a public announcements system. Scientists should study this camp's grapevine; it's probably a clue to breaking the speed of light. Yes, those pictures. Did the gossip say anything more about them?"

"I gather they were extremely unpleasant." Renzi edited out some comments he'd heard along the lines of "screaming nightmares."

"Understatement of the year! Mavros has gotten even worse since he picked up Angelos – Angel of Death, he calls himself. What they did to those poor, dumb supply train guards they captured –" Gabrel shook his head. "The colonel's right, he has to be put down. And we need to do it now, before he grows stronger, or prepare for a bloody civil war. He's not just being sadistic, you know. He really is what the Harmonicas call us – a terrorist. And he's gaining forces; there will always be some people who just want to join up with whoever they perceive as strongest, and some who are too afraid of his retaliation to refuse the invitation."

"Mm. I see why the colonel wants his most brilliant tactician on the job."

"What?" Gabrel looked startled. "He didn't mention bringing in anyone else."

Renzi punched him lightly on the arm. "I meant *you*, idiot."

"Oh yeah? Well the 'brilliant tactician' hasn't yet worked out how to obliterate three dozen armed men with a force barely two-thirds of that. Damn it, I wish I hadn't given him a share of the new blasters. That's fifteen small arms he didn't have before. And he had just over twenty men at that point. At least his new followers won't have blasters." Gabrel's steps slowed and he scowled out over the camp below them. "Renzi, I've never done a pitched battle. I do quick in-and-out raids, harassing tactics, morale destroyers. I know how to piss Mavros off but not how to destroy him."

"You'll figure it out," Renzi said. "But I guess that rules out the favor I was going to ask you."

"Why, what was it?"

"To steal a printer for me... just a little one, a 2D job. Though I guess it's not so urgent, if we're not going to be leafletting the Harmonicas any more."

"I thought you had a printer, you've certainly been coming up with enough propaganda leaflets."

"Had," Renzi said, "is the operative world. That damned girl you offloaded onto us!"

"*Isovel?* Oh, I guess I shouldn't be surprised. She tried to sabotage the small-arms printer we liberated from the army. Wasn't successful, though."

"That's probably because you weren't fool enough to let her try and 'fix' it."

"Oh. Oh, Renzi, you didn't!" Gabrel laughed and sounded ten years younger. "You do know you are never going to live this down?"

Renzi scowled. "That damned girl. The colonel was brilliant to trade her for concessions from the enemy. Me, I'd have *paid* them to take her back."

"Yep. She never stopped thinking of ways to trip us up, did she? Spirited girl. Brave, too." Gabrel's voice softened in a way that alarmed Renzi.

"Gabrel. That… that *snake* didn't get to you too?"

"Too?"

"She's gone to the heads of half our officers. I thought you would have better sense."

"You've got to admit that her initiative is admirable. You're just annoyed because she exercised it on their side instead of ours."

"And there's no fixing that. I showed her the Library – would you believe she'd never seen a paper book before? – suggested readings, explained stuff to her…"

"Um. Sounds as if she went to your head too. Don't worry, I'm not jealous. She's hard to resist."

"Never!" Renzi recoiled. "I'd as soon bed a viper. But I did think she was coming round to understand our side."

"That," said Gabrel slowly, "is one of the things I find so admirable. Even if she did begin to see that we have a side, nothing would shake her sense of duty towards her own."

"Stubborn. A troublemaker. Destructive. Whatever did you see in that –"

"Renzi, don't say anything that'll oblige me to hit you."

They'd come around the track to the view over the camp again. Renzi slowed, came to a halt and looked out into the gathering darkness. There, among the dark angular shapes of tents and the moving points of light, was the best of Esilia. How could Gabrel be infatuated with someone who wanted to destroy them?

"We may have a temporary truce that allows their army to withdraw," he said finally, "but, Gabrel, she's still on the other side. That's not something you can fix."

"Oh... I don't know. If there's a peace treaty, there won't be two sides any more, will there?"

"So you're going to waste your time hoping that happens?"

"I suppose I'll just have to make it happen."

Renzi snorted. "I'd forgotten your breathtaking modesty. You and what army?"

"Me and --" Gabrel broke off and drew a long breath. "Ha! It might work. It just might. Renzi, thank you. I've had an idea about the Karamanlis problem."

"What?"

"Tell you if it works out."

* * *

Rauf Dayvson's eyes widened briefly in surprise at the proposal from his unexpected visitor. To gain time, he took off the glasses that Isovel insisted he wear to reduce eyestrain and polished the lenses with a handkerchief.

They were seated on camp stools outside his tent, where he could command privacy for the conversation without giving this strange young man an opportunity to assassinate him – if that was the real reason behind this visit. Dayvson thought it unlikely – for one thing, it would be a suicide mission – but he wouldn't put anything past the insurgents.

Without the glasses, he saw the terrain before them as a gentle blur of water and stone stretching downward from the camping spot. The rushing green waters of the river blended with the paler green of lichens and moss on the eroded limestone that bordered and constrained the water. He could only tell where the stone left off and the water began by the dazzling sparkles of sun that danced on the surface of the waters.

It made more sense than the near view. Dayvson slid the glasses back on and looked at the rebel who had come uninvited, under a flag of truce, with his outrageous proposal.

"We may have agreed to a temporary truce," he gently reminded his visitor, "but we are still at war. The Central Committee would have my head if I agreed to joint operations with the enemy forces – and they'd be right."

The young man calling himself Captain Gabrel Moresco leaned forward, elbows on the table. "From what I hear, they may well call for your head anyway. It's not your fault that you were sent into these hills with inadequate logistic support, untrained men, and no experience in counter-insurgency tactics. And you've adapted amazingly fast; in the last week before the truce, we Free Esilians were finding it much more difficult to attack the column. But most likely you'll pay the price for a generally unsuccessful campaign."

"And you're here to help me. Now I've heard everything!"

"Not specifically to help you, no. Let's say that I'm here to point out some areas where we both want the same thing."

"How is that even possible?" How dare this disheveled young man even talk about "joint operations" of the Expeditionary Force with his rag-tag gang of misfits and terrorists? They didn't even have proper uniforms, and this particular guerrilla leader had probably awarded himself the rank of captain because it sounded good.

"Consider the long term. If Harmony wins this war, you or someone like you will have to deal with the Karamanlis gang, and they'll be that much stronger and more powerful by then; he'll have half the hill villages controlled under his reign of terror. If, on the other hand, Esilia wins its independence, we'll either have to grant Karamanlis' demands for a major role in the new government, or follow the peace with a civil war. I may not be here in the long term, General, and you may not either, but it is in both our nations' interest to put down this bunch of sadistic bandits before they grow stronger."

He had a point. "Without in any way accepting your description of the Penal Colony as a 'nation,' I do agree that it is in everyone's interest to defeat this group as soon as possible. The notion of allowing them a voice in government, though, is absolutely untenable."

Gabrel Moresco looked amused. "Yes, well, if you win the war then Esilia will still be managed from Harmony City, so there won't be any local government for Mavros Karamanlis to demand a share in." For the fifth or sixth time, he glanced to his left, where Dayvson's staff officers waited well out of earshot. Behind them streamed the soldiers, tents, supplies and support personnel of the Harmony Expedition Force. They might have lost an unnerving number of men to the insurgents' raids, but what remained was still enough to impress this Captain Moresco with the might of Harmony.

He hoped.

"In the short term, General, a decisive victory over Mavros Karamanlis would do much to bolster your position with Harmony.

And surely you must wish to take revenge on him. After all, it was your soldiers that he tortured and killed."

Dayvson could not help but recall Andrus' wearying harping on the public-relations need for some victory.

"And your short-term benefits? And stop looking over my army," Dayvson added, "or I'll conclude that this whole proposal is just a ruse to allow you a close-up look about my forces and dispositions."

"You overrate me, General, if you think I can just glance at your army and come up with better information than our scouts have already given me. If I'm looking at them too often, well, you must admit it's an impressive sight. Do you find it difficult to have your family in the line of march?"

The non sequitur surprised Rauf. "What does that have to do with your proposition?"

"Oh, nothing, nothing. I was just wondering if your daughter's presence made you unwilling to close with the Karamanlis gang. I can certainly understand –"

"My daughter," Rauf Dayvson said stiffly, "is hardly your concern."

"Does she march with you and the staff officers, or back in the baggage train?"

"That," said Dayvson, "is also not your concern. And I notice that you changed the subject as soon as I asked how you personally would benefit from the proposed operation."

"With respect, General, I believe it was you who changed the subject." Moresco's eyes flicked towards the army again. "As for short term benefits – I'm not the one who needs a public-relations coup. It is enough of a benefit for me to see this filth cleansed from my country. And, of course, not getting my men killed is a bonus."

"So you'd get mine killed instead!"

"I believe this proposal minimizes the danger to either of our forces." Gabrel traced an irregular line across the top of the table. "Suppose this is the course of the river. Karamanlis has struck here, here and here." His forefinger stabbed at the site of the supply train attack and at two other places somewhere east of the Vanyan. "Your army is not very good at hunting down insurgents, no criticism implied, it's our territory and we know it better. Our forces are only lightly armed and have no experience in fighting a conventional battle; we learned that at Dun Valley. I propose to station my people at strategic points behind Karamanlis and to drive him towards the river, where your infantry and artillery can dispose of him." A brief flashing grin. "After all, he too has no experience of conventional warfare. If you can trap him between the Vanyan and our people, you should be able to mop his gang up without breaking a sweat."

Damn it, the boy made sense. "Prisoners?"

"We don't take them. Use your own judgment. Personally, having seen the pictures of his latest work, I'd favor killing them all. And whatever you do, be sure to kill Angelos Thanatu."

Dayvson had picked up a little of the local dialect. "Angel of Death?"

"That's what he calls himself. Slight, golden haired, face like an angel. And largely responsible for turning Mavros' gang from an undisciplined bunch of bandits into an organized force of terror. We'll kill him if we get a chance; if not, it'll be up to you."

Dayvson drummed his fingers on the table top, trying to think. "I don't know..."

"Would you like to discuss it with your staff officers? I don't mind waiting."

"Discord, no!" He was beginning to see a way in which this could be managed with much less risk to him – but it would be best if nobody else knew about it beforehand. "If I did agree to this hair-brained scheme, how were you planning to coordinate operations with us?"

"I'm not. All you have to do is make camp at the place I suggest, stay there overnight, and have your men ready at first light. We'll be tracking your progress; whenever you get there, we'll flush Karamanlis out and herd him towards the river."

"The place?"

"You marched through a relatively wide valley on the way here. Remember the place where two black stones lean toward one another? Right after that the river valley opens out for a short while; there's more room for conventional forces to form up than you'd find anywhere else before you're back in the foothills."

Dayvson remembered that landmark quite clearly, largely because so many of the soldiers had been spooked by it. Somebody – maybe the man in front of him – had started a rumor that the two tall stones were the Old Gods of the land and would crush anyone who came to conquer. Nonsense, of course. He'd made a point of having his tent pitched immediately beneath the place where the stones leaned out from the cliff, and made another point of telling everyone how well he'd slept there.

Reasonably well, anyway.

The annoying little showers of pebbles that had recurred during that night were merely coincidental.

"Done," he said, with a sinking feeling that he had just jumped off a cliff and discovered that the river was a long way down. "I'll position my people there, and *if* you can deliver Karamanlis we'll deal with him."

That decision made, he saw the rebel "officer" off as quickly as possible, and without giving him the chance he clearly desired to hang about the camp and chat with the other officers. A very strange young man indeed, he thought. He seemed to switch from intense focus on the war to pointless blathering and social inanities about his family. Well, it wasn't his problem. He didn't have to disclose the deal unless the rebels actually came through. He could tell his staff officers that a scout had reported guerrillas moving towards the river just south of Black Rocks and that he wanted the troops ready to attack. If the rebels didn't deliver Karamanlis, it would just be a case of bad information and he wouldn't discuss their idea of a joint attack.

Isovel was acting peculiar, too. She had blazed with excitement when he mentioned Moresco's visit, and he'd hoped she was for once showing an intelligent curiosity about the course of the war; then when he explained how he'd sent the fellow about his business, she seemed to lose interest all at once. Naturally, he couldn't tell her about their agreement; women always talked, they couldn't help it.

He would have to make sure she was well out of the way at Black Rocks. Women were a confounded nuisance to an army on the march; the sooner she was back in his quarters in Colony City, where she belonged, the happier he'd be. And this time she wasn't going to have access to a flitter.

CHAPTER EIGHTEEN

Governor's Mansion, Colony City, Esilia: four months later

Gabrel looked appreciatively at the linen-fold wood paneling and the collection of Esilian paintings hung just above the paneling. Stark desert scenes in red and ochre, with sharp purple shadows, alternated with artists' conceptions of the mountains. True, most of the latter showed that very few artists bothered to actually go to the mountains; they showed gently rolling hills rising to a distant horizon rather than jagged peaks and stony valleys from which you never saw the horizon. But there was one small painting of a girl with a doat on a string, in front of a low-ceilinged stone house, that showed some actual feeling for the land.

"Governor Aberforss was a connoisseur of your native art," the uniformed man on the other side of the table informed Gabrel. He was flanked by other officers, but none of them seemed willing to venture on conversation. "Fortunately, the staff never got around to implementing Governor Serman's orders to have all these pictures stored in the attic or, better, sold. It would be a pity to break up the collection, would it not?"

"Indeed." Although if the Harmonicas did sell off the paintings, Gabrel just might put in a bid for that smallish one.

He saw that General Dayvson had acquired several new decorations since they last met. Evidently the Battle of Black Rocks had burnished his reputation. And yet, and yet… He and Colonel Travis and two other officers were here to discuss the terms on which Harmony would consent to withdraw troops and recognize the nation of Esilia. So that one victory hadn't been enough to stem the anti-war sentiment in Harmony.

"And how is your political officer doing?" Colonel Travis asked. "Given his role in establishing communications, I had thought to see him here."

The general frowned. "Recalled to Harmony City. The Committee felt he had overstepped his privilege. Discord, *I* felt Andrus had overstepped his privilege, but I wasn't about to send him home for doing something that worked. He got my daughter back and negotiated the terms that led to our victory at Black Rocks. I owe him.

"This is his replacement, Kolin Shiflet." Dayvson indicated the one un-decorated man on his side of the table and closed his mouth with a definite air of wanting to say more than was advisable in a room about to be connected with the Central Committee.

That killed that line of conversation. But there wasn't much for any of them to do until the connection with Harmony went live. The silence was uncomfortable, and Dayvson had already ordered kahve for everyone. Gabrel racked his brains for some kind of neutral small talk and was relieved when Dayvson started a new topic.

"How is your second – Patrik, wasn't it?" he asked Gabrel. "A most impressive young man. Of course, all of your people were a great help; your taking out Karamanlis' men from their rear distracted and slowed them enough for us to whip green troops back into formation. But Patrik was…"

"Impressive? Impressively foolhardy?" Gabrel suggested. Patrik had been an idiot, exposing himself time after time to kill or harass the enemy guerrillas. "One of the Karamanlis gang sliced his belly open. Fortunately, the gut wasn't pierced; he's been making a long convalescence in the hills." He had also been the subject of several epic songs and the object of the village girls' adoration; Gabrel might never be able to punish him appropriately for risking his life so casually. "And your aide-de-camp? Kamron, wasn't it?"

"Secretary," Dayvson corrected him. "Discording fool, he was supposed to take shelter with the other noncombatants. But he'd seen those pictures… He picked up a blaster from a fallen grunt and went wide to stop some men who were trying to sneak upriver to flank us. Of course he couldn't do it, he'd had next to no military training, it wasn't a job for one man. But his action alerted us to the threat. He received several awards." Dayvson cleared his throat. "Posthumously."

The screen on the right-hand wall flickered with light and Dayvson cleared his throat again. "Well, here we go. I've been studying treaties from ancient wars- "

"Captain Moresco and Lieutenant Renzi have been researching the same subject." Colonel Travis told him. "I suppose we'll just have to make it up as we go along."

Dayvson nodded. "Much as we fought the war. Do you know, I'm getting tired of being thrown feet-first into 'learning experiences.' It'll be a relief to go back to telling students to examine the root causes and long-term results of the Gallic Wars."

Several hours and half a gallon of black kahve later, the screen showing the Central Committee flickered off and the men sitting around the table stretched. After a moment of silence Dayvson volunteered, "Well, we have reached consensus on *some* issues."

"Yes. The time for the next meeting." Colonel Travis yawned. Gabrel clamped his mouth shut to keep from doing the same.

"An indefinite cease-fire. Repatriation of prisoners. Governor Serman to be replaced." Dayvson was determinedly cheerful.

"Don't count that last among your consensus items. *We* didn't ask for Serman to be replaced."

"You asked for him to be removed. Same thing."

"No. We will not accept another governor from Harmony."

"Oh, come now. This colony doesn't run itself. You need somebody at the top to provide governance and to represent you to Harmony."

Travis sighed. "We will – well, I don't feel the need to explain the details of our plan for self-government. All we really want is for Harmony to recognize us as an independent country – and to get out of the way."

The political officer sneered. "Dreams! You need to accept that Harmony will never grant you independence, and start bargaining for what you can actually get."

"If you people don't grant us independence, we'll take it. And your time is limited. I'm not sure how long I can hold back my victorious forces from attacking Colony City."

The meeting broke up among snarls of acrimony.

"Not very hopeful," said Gabrel as he and the colonel strolled towards the sweeping marble stairs, trailed by Renzi and the colonel's aide-de-camp. Dayvson and the political had availed themselves of the elevator.

Travis bared his teeth. "On the contrary. They're already squabbling amongst themselves. By next time factions will have developed – But we shouldn't discuss my plans here. And don't you have something else to do?"

Gabrel nodded acquiescence and slipped away from the other three, melting into the shadows of the statuary that lined the hall.

"Captain Moresco?" Travis repeated when General Dayvson met him at the foot of the stairs. "I believe he went in search of your, ah, facilities. He drank a lot of kahve during the meeting."

"That shouldn't take long."

"Perhaps he lost his way, not being accustomed to such a spacious and elegant house. Very few Esilians visited here during Wilyam Serman's term of office." Colonel Travis glanced at his wrist chrono. "Rather a scatter-brained young man. I can't wait for him; I'm due at our own headquarters in a few minutes. If you find him wandering around, please direct him to the door and tell him I said to take a commercial flitter back."

Gabrel slipped quietly through the shadowed rooms on the rest of the top floor, trapping inconspicuous metallic burrs in draperies or on the backs of upholstered chairs. With only a few minutes in hand, he didn't take the time to decide which rooms, aside from the meeting room – where he had already left his little gifts – would be the most use to bug.

He did pause on opening the door to a bedroom lined with pale green draperies. A glint of gold sparkled at the folds of the curtains. He took a deep breath of the air. Essence of Isovel – but she wasn't there.

Time to go downstairs.

* * *

Seated in the small windowed room on the ground floor, Isovel had left the door ajar so that she could catch a glimpse of the Esilian negotiating party when they came down the grand marble stairs. A shadow fell across the floor just outside the open door and she caught her breath. But it was only one of the native servants.

"You have a caller, Miss Isovel. Shall I stay while you receive him?"

"No! I mean – that's not necessary, Shila. He's an old friend. Just show him in." Her heart was beating ridiculously fast. *I will come for you.* Except he hadn't done that when he made that dangerous visit to her father to propose a combined operation; he hadn't even spoken to her. She shouldn't get her hopes up now. Especially since –

Her caller was Jonny Kelso, and he closed the door behind him. She looked him over. He was, naturally, just as tall as ever, with those blue eyes glowing under the thick yellow hair that the military had forced him to keep far too short. It wasn't too short now; he'd let it grow out and someone had coaxed its natural curl into a becoming slanted line across his forehead. His civilian clothes were also becoming; well fitted without being tight, they showed off his broad shoulders and muscular arms.

Six months ago she'd probably have been fanning herself at the mere sight. Now she concealed her disappointment and greeted him politely. But as an old acquaintance. Not as the love of her life.

He looked – *relieved?* at her cool, civil greeting. What was going on there? And how was she going to break the news to him that their brief, mad affair was over? *I knew this was coming. I should have made plans.* But like an idiot, she'd been mooning over Gabrel.

"I, um, just got demobbed," Jonny said awkwardly.

"Your hair certainly grew fast." You didn't go from buzz cut to carefully combed dark gold curls in a day. Or a week for that matter.

"Yes, well, ain't just so easy to get to see you. What with you living in the Governor's mansion and all. Now that I don't work here."

But today he'd just walked in and announced himself, hadn't he? What was he not saying?

"I'm glad to see you're all right," she said finally. *Not that I ever bothered to make sure. I am pond scum.* "I was afraid those rebels might have hurt you."

Jonny's perfectly shaped lips curved. "Only my dignity. I was more afraid for *you*. 'T'was a great day when I heard you'd escaped the rebels."

She hadn't exactly escaped. She'd been *traded*. Which didn't do a lot for her dignity, so she should be grateful that the newsers had broadcast an account of her kidnapping and return that was, well, a very pretty fiction.

"Well." The need to break up with him was a very large Awkwardness sitting in the middle of this small room. For some reason she visualized it as a huge ostrich. With bad breath. "How – how have you been?"

A crooked smile. "Your dad was not best pleased that I'd allowed you to be captured."

"It wasn't exactly your fault."

"He didn't see't that way. D'you know, he had a stockade built just for me 'n my buddies?"

"No! Is that where you've been all this time?"

"Nah, he cooled down after he got through all the planning t'invade the mountains. Found us some work to do here. Told us t'report to Lieutenant Nusom. Dunno what *he* did to piss your dad off, but he's in charge of maintaining the city sewage system. All of us coming from Harmony strained the system some, y'know. Lots of blockages t'clear."

"Oh. Ugh. Jonny, I'm so sorry!"

"Nah, somebody had t'do it. And I met some real nice folks, civilians y'know? This girl – Tiffni – she worked in her dad's food truck, right opposite Lieutenant Nusom's office. Used to give us end-of-day leftovers. And she was some cook!" Jonny's accent wasn't so thick now that he was thinking more about his story than about his exalted surroundings. "*Real* nice girl. Didn't hate us like a lot of the natives. We used to talk, some, about the war. She understood I didn't have no choice, had to go where the draft sent me. And she taught me a lot about Esilia."

Footsteps on the marble stairs outside; a confusion of masculine voices making "goodbye" noises. Isovel was listening so hard, she barely realized when Jonny stopped talking.

"Oh!" He'd been saying nice things about this Tiffni, hadn't he? "Should I call on her and thank her for helping you through a difficult time?"

"No!" Jonny swallowed. "She, uh, doesn't know about you. We just told her we was on punishment detail for being drunk on duty."

A beautiful thought spread through Isovel's mind. "Jonny. Did you come here to break up with me?"

"Gentleman doesn't do that to a lady. Just though you sh'd know…" The sentence died in his throat while he stared at the draperies over her head.

"Know what?" Isovel prodded gently when it seemed he was at a complete standstill.

It came out in an unhappy rush. "I'd ruther be with Tiffni than with you."

Isovel tried not to laugh. Evidently her expression made Jonny think she was trying to hold back tears. "Isovel, don't cry! I didn't want t'hurt you. You *knew* we couldn't last – a grunt and the general's daughter? Now Tiffni, her dad doesn't mind me. He said if I stay after the war, he'll take me into the business, he's been wanting to expand to two food trucks…"

"It sounds like an opportunity you should definitely seize, Jonny. Don't feel bad for me; I'll go back to Harmony, you know, and I'll always remember our time together as a pleasant dream." Apart from the last night, which had been more of a nightmare. "I wish you and Tiffni all the best. Ah, we don't yet know the terms of the peace treaty. If we grant Esilia independence, can you legally stay here, or will you need some help with the formalities?"

Jonny turned red. "Tiffni's dad says they're sure to get independence. And he says Esilia always welcomes new settlers, and they've been taking in a lot of deserters anyway."

The footsteps and voices outside the room had ceased, and no one had tapped at the door. Isovel's heart sank. But she mustn't show that to Jonny; he would think she was grieving over losing him. She put on her brilliant society smile. "Then all you need from me is my best wishes to you and Tiffni, which you already have." *Go away and let me be miserable in private.*

"Are you sure you'll be all right, Izzy?"

Another bright smile. "Oh, you know how shallow I am. I declare, I quite lost my heart to a dashing rebel officer in the mountains!"

Jonny snorted. "As if *you* of all people would fall for a rebel! I expect he was just an amusement while you was sitting around being a bored hostage."

"I expect so." *No, I was an amusement for* him. "Goodbye, Jonny."

"Goodbye, Izzy."

She waited until the sound of his boots had faded away before sinking down on a sofa, hands clenched. Because she was *not* going to cry over a man who hadn't even bothered to show up to break with her. Who had forgotten his promise to come for her. Who –

"Izzy. I like that. It sounds so much more approachable than Isovel. I think I'll call you Izzy from now on."

She jumped up and whirled towards the mocking voice. Gabrel Moresco was standing beside a long ruffled curtain that was still moving slightly. "*How did you get in here?*"

"Walked in," Gabrel said. "You two seemed somewhat preoccupied; I didn't want to disturb anything."

"But Shila should have announced you!"

"Shila? Would that be the pretty little girl who flutters around your front hall? I think she was distracted by all the other officers leaving. Especially Renzi. You know, that's just what he needs, a nice, pliable little girl who will think everything he says is brilliant."

"Indeed? I wouldn't know."

"No, that wouldn't have occurred to you. Seeing that you are not nice." He took a step towards her. "Or pliable." Another step. "Or particularly little." He closed the distance between them and took her in his arms. "What a good thing that I'm susceptible to sarcastic women who are as tall as I am. Of course, it helps if they're beautiful. And have a cloud of fair hair that tends to come down when they're agitated."

Isovel felt the hair falling around her face as he spoke. And one of his hands was moving close to her head. "Cheater. I am *not* agitated. You're taking my hairpins out!"

"As you told me once -that's not what your pulse says," Gabrel murmured. "Admit it. You're happy to see me come courting you."

Isovel brought up her own hands and pushed lightly against his chest. Immediately he let her go and moved back a step.

And she was *not* disappointed that he let her go so easily. It was all of a piece with his earlier behavior. Which she could bring to mind more clearly now that he was not actually touching her.

"What, your idea of courting is to drop in on a girl every few months to build up your ego?"

Gabrel looked wounded. "I have been busy with a few other matters. Encouraging Harmony to give up on an expensive and divisive war. Helping Colonel Travis with his plans to make a nation out of a colony. Do you realize we have no administrative structure of our own? Everything was run by bureaucrats imported from Harmony."

Isovel sat back down. "I see. Aren't you being a touch premature? Peace negotiations only began this morning."

"We'll get our independence."

"You sound as confident as Tiffni's father."

"I – who?"

So he hadn't been listening to the whole conversation. Just the last few sentences. "Soon to be Jonny's father-in-law, I imagine. And future food truck king of Colony City."

Gabrel shook his head. "You people have *no* gift for names. You make everything sound as appealing as a shopping list. I'm surprised you don't just number your cities and natural landmarks. City 1, City 2…"

Isobel choked back a laugh. "Please don't suggest that to the Central Committee. They might think it was a brilliant idea!"

"I see. But however delightful it is to wander through this garden of bright images, are you not forgetting a subject of almost equal importance?"

"*What?*"

"Ah, you have not encountered Kai Lung. Or even Dorothy Sayers. Well, there'll be plenty of time to improve your education…. Tell me more about this dashing rebel officer to whom you lost your heart."

He *would* have been in time to overhear that line. Naturally. Isovel tried for a light tinkling laugh. It didn't quite come off. "If you were listening, you also know that I'm shallow and a desperate flirt. I may have relieved the boredom of being a hostage with a light flirtation, but evidently the attraction – on both sides – was not strong enough to survive a few months' separation."

"Oh?"

"The man said he would come for me. But the one time that he came, he talked to my father about military matters and didn't even speak to me – not even to say good-bye."

"Oh, for the Black Gods' sake, *Izzy.* I hinted all over the place until I sounded a complete fool, but your father refused to hear the hints. And I could hardly come right out and request permission to see you. Remember, I was on the wrong side then."

"Aren't you still on the wrong side?"

Gabrel waved a hand. "Eh, it's all over but the details. Hostilities have already ceased, Harmony is going to recognize us as an independent state, and in the future there will be only one side – the side of peace."

"You're very confident."

"About that, yes. About other things… I asked once if you would consider staying in Esilia, but my timing was abominable. Of course you had to return to your father, it was part of the treaty. But now… Have you had time to give the matter any thought?"

"Until today I didn't know I needed to! You'd disappeared!"

"I too had duties." Uninvited, he took a seat beside her on the couch. Much closer than necessary; it was a generously built piece of furniture. He didn't *have* to crowd against her, to stretch out one lean leg to touch hers all the way down, to put one arm around her shoulders.

It was extraordinarily comfortable. Her traitor body felt that it had come home at last, that 'home' was wherever Gabrel happened to be. Isovel put out of her mind the considerations the Political Officer had dinned into her and tried to simply enjoy the moment.

"There is really a lot to be said for staying in Esilia," Gabrel told her. "For one thing, here you could take all the applied math and science courses you liked – had you thought about that? And don't you think it would be exhilarating to see a new nation being built?"

"I think," Isovel said honestly, "that building a nation would involve a lot of very long meetings and a lot of you working 15 hours a day and coming home exhausted."

"Ah, but if I had somebody to come home to I wouldn't work such long hours."

"I don't believe that for a moment," Isovel said, "any more than I believe a bunch of Esilians can stop arguing long enough to achieve harmony."

"Yes, well, there are other ways to proceed besides sitting in meetings until everybody has been browbeaten into supporting the chairman's views. Like winning the argument." He dipped his head and kissed her lightly on the lips. "Between two people, though, I'll admit that consensus is highly desirable." His lips grazed her jaw line and moved on to her neck. "*I* am firmly of the opinion that you should stay in Esilia. What do you think?"

"I can't think at all when you're doing that!" She pushed his head away from her collarbone before he could venture farther.

And, discord it, now she remembered all of Political Officer Shiflet's lectures.

"I still have responsibilities here. My father –"

"Esilians," Gabrel said, "still have the quaint belief that it's for the parent to take care of the child, not vice versa."

"Oh, hush up. You don't understand: it's all political. Harmony may be tired of war, but that doesn't mean they're happy about the prospect of withdrawing their troops and having spent so much for no gain." *When did* Harmony *become* they? "They will be looking for a scapegoat to blame, and one of the easy choices will be to blame my father for incompetence and claim that it was only his blunders that made it impossible to carry on with the war. When we get home, Shiflet says he'll be *that* close," she held up her thumb and forefinger, all but touching, "to a show trial and public disgrace. He can't survive the public relations disaster of his daughter staying in Esilia and, worse, marrying a rebel leader. Half the newsers will say I rejected him for his bumbling misconduct and the other half will say it proves that he was colluding with the enemy from the beginning."

"That's – ah – a very quick political analysis."

"The new Political Officer has been lecturing me for weeks. After Andrus briefed him, he was certain you were going to come to Colony City and try to seduce me. Of course I told him not to worry, you'd forgotten all about me."

"You couldn't have said I was too honorable to seduce you?"

"Oh, shut up." Isovel took his face between her hands and kissed him. "I have to go back to Harmony with Daddy." She buried her own face in the crook of his neck. "I have to be seen to be standing by him in this moment of crisis," she said into his shoulder. "It's my duty." His shirt would blot up the tears welling out of her eyes.

Gabrel sighed deeply. "I wish you really were a shallow, frivolous girl living for the moment. You'd be much easier to manage."

"You wouldn't love me if I were that girl."

Gabrel took hold of her shoulders and forced her up to face him. "So you do understand that I love you?"

Isovel nodded and bit her lower lip to keep it from trembling.

"And I would love you wherever we met and whatever you were doing. If you were a flibberty-gibbet of a teenager or a scolding spinster, you would still be my only love." He lifted the mass of her hair with one hand. "My quarrelsome, difficult, insanely loyal love. Well, if you must return to Harmony…"

"In a year or two the situation might not be so tense," Isobel offered. "I might be able – of course it's not fair to you, asking you to wait on something you can't control."

"Yes," Gabrel said, sounding distant already. "I do prefer things I can control. So here's a promise: I *will* come for you. If *you* can wait."

"But you can't –"

He stopped her mouth with a kiss. "You would be *amazed* at what I can do. Remember, you're talking to the man who organized a cooperative action between the insurgents and the army that was supposed to put them down. And that was when we were still at war. Once peace has been agreed upon, there will be much more scope for creativity." He paused. "It may take a little while. We have a lot of work to do. But in the meantime… well. I won't ask you to have faith in me. But promise that you won't get married without giving me a chance to forbid the banns."

217

Isobel sniffed and tried to chuckle. "You haven't got much to worry about."

"Oh? Because no other man could possibly attract you, now that you've known *me*?"

Damn the man. He was manipulating her into laughing. "I'm not going to build up your ego that much! I just don't imagine that somebody who's been in such notorious fixes, from sleeping with a private to staying all alone with a group of desperate rebels and – it really doesn't bear thinking about, dear, what they might have done to her!" She ended with a pretty good imitation of a society matron gossiping to a crony. "I doubt I'll be besieged with suitors!"

"I wish I shared your confidence," Gabrel said. "I wish I could persuade you not to show anyone your profile, or look at a man with your very fine eyes, or let them glimpse your glorious hair. Oh, and if you could wear dowdy, ill-fitting outfits, that would help."

"Idiot. You can't *make* smartcloth fit badly."

"You could try!"

And he was off while she was laughing, not even waiting for a last kiss.

Which would probably, despite all his castles in the air, be the last time she ever kissed him.

And she'd lost out on it because the wretched man had made her laugh.

* * *

"Your victorious forces, eh?"

Gabrel and Colonel Travis were pacing back and forth in the small garden attached to the building that had been requisitioned for the Esilians, on the theory that open air and movement would thwart the bugs with which the house was probably riddled.

The colonel smiled. "We don't need to get into where they are, or how long it might take me to collect them. No point confusing the Harmonicas with irrelevant details, eh?"

"None at all."

"Sadly, it will take more than the stick to get them to a treaty. We need to apply the carrot as well. I tried to explain that both our countries would be richer if Esilia were a free and independent trading partner. They seem impervious to that logic. Can they really not get that we'll will be much more inventive and innovative if we're allowed to work for ourselves? And that as our only on-planet trading partner, they'll benefit too?"

"Judging from my experience with one Harmonica," Gabrel said, "it takes a long, long time to persuade them that coercion isn't the way to get the best out of people."

It was a depressing thought.

CHAPTER NINETEEN

⟶ ⟵

The meetings to hammer out details of a peace treaty that would allow both sides to claim victory became Gabrel's new standard for boredom. General Dayvson was recalled to Harmony and Isovel, naturally, went with him. The general was replaced as chief negotiator with a political officer several levels senior to Shiflet, a direct representative of the Central Committee.

Harmony's government had been conceived in the spirit of consensus. Gabrel had occasionally wondered how a government could accomplish anything at all if the representatives spent all their time debating until they achieved consensus. Now he found out. The Central Committee had redefined consensus as, "We agree with the Head of Committee, and everybody else agrees with us."

It did not make for smooth negotiations.

"Of course it takes forever," Gabrel exploded to Renzi one day as they were walking back from the Governor's Mansion. "How can we work out a treaty with people who don't even have the concept of negotiating? Their entire government works on a basis of 'do as you're told,' and they can't figure out how to talk to anybody who doesn't accept that model."

That whole morning had been wasted on a series of 'ultimatums' from the Central Committee. Colonel Travis, imperturbable as usual, had politely met each ultimatum with an explanation that Esilia considered itself a sovereign state and was no longer bound by the decisions of the Committee. "I don't know how the colonel keeps his temper. I wanted to set the chief political officer's beard on fire."

Renzi's lips twitched. "I suspect Colonel Travis would say that you are the very model of a firebrand and should not be entrusted with any diplomatic task."

"Oh, he's ahead of you there. Do you know why I never say anything during these meetings? I am not permitted to speak. His orders."

"Hmm. You've always been a slippery, twisty devil with a gift for getting your own way. What's your problem this time?"

Gabrel glared at his friend. "I'm good at making *reasonable* people see *reason*. That doesn't apply here. I don't know why we have to sit through these interminable meetings. You never say anything either."

"I suspect you're there to force them to look at the face of the man who nibbled away at their invading army until they gave up. To remind them that a boy of twenty-three outsmarted their general and all his staff. Repeatedly."

"I'm twenty-four now," Gabrel said stiffly. "Not exactly a 'boy.'"

"Well, you're going to like my second theory even less."

"Which is?"

"We're being groomed to become the colonel's personal assistants after the treaty is signed. Turning Esilia from a colony into a nation is going to involve a level of work that will make these meetings look like a vacation on the beach. Sitting through the meetings gets us up to speed on a lot of the issues Travis will have to deal with."

"Issues." Gabrel kicked a pebble out of his way. "I'm *not* a damned *politician*. There are lots of people better qualified."

"But you," Renzi said, "are the face of the insurgency."

"Why me?" Gabrel all but howled. "All I did was follow the colonel's orders." He lofted a somewhat larger cobblestone with the toe of his boot.

"Um. The orders were, 'Harass the enemy at your discretion,' and you followed them with great initiative and inventiveness. I suspect he plans to turn you loose on our new country's issues in much the same way. He'll say, 'We need an independent judiciary,' and you'll come up with a book-length position paper describing which types of judges should be appointed, which ones elected, how their powers can be kept separate from the legislative and executive branches, and names of suitable candidates."

"Sounds more like you than me."

"I expect it'll take both of us." Renzi sounded infuriatingly calm. "I may not be a Hero of the Revolution, but after maintaining the colonel's copy of the library and encouraging people to get acquainted with it, I have an encyclopedic knowledge of the contents. And the Reference Library is the closest thing we have to a How-to-Build-a-Nation manual."

"I. Can. Hardly. Wait. Ow!" Gabrel had found a rock too well wedged into the street to respond to his kick.

* * *

Renzi's predictions were all too accurate. Gabrel had been hoping to take a long enough leave to visit Harmony once the countries were formally at peace; instead, the work of hammering out a treaty

223

merged directly into the work of creating a nation. Colonel Travis had secretaries to do the grunt work and expert senior advisers on the topics that obviously needed work, but he said that he couldn't do without his two young aides to whip up emergency position papers, liaise with expert advisers, and perform all sorts of irregular tasks. "In practice," Renzi said cheerfully, "that means we rush all around the enterprise applying duck tape."

"What's duck tape?"

"Um… I don't actually know. It doesn't have anything to do with ducks, I don't think. But there's a saying, 'Duck tape is the force that binds the universe together.' I think we are Colonel Travis' duck tape."

"*Not* my highest aim in life."

"Oh, I don't know." The colonel's praise had lifted the final shadow of guilt over Renzi's performance during the actual fighting. Now he thought of himself as "Young Man on the Way Up," rather than "Pathetic Failure." Gabrel had thought that would make his friend easier to live with, but at times Sunny Optimistic Renzi could be just as irritating as Desperately Depressed Renzi. Right now, for instance, he was happily enumerating the subjects on which they'd have both expertise and inside knowledge after Colonel Travis' work was done.

"I never realized how different a colony was from an independent nation."

"I know," said Gabrel glumly. "Even I thought we would just kick the Harmonicas out and go on as we had been doing."

"Instead, we're getting an inside view of the birth of a nation. Last week Colonel Travis had me writing position papers on the franchise and the choice of which offices should be elective and which run by appointees."

"Obviously, they should all be elective."

"Gabrel, think for a moment. Whoever becomes Prime Minister shouldn't have to staff his Cabinet with elected officials; they'd inevitably pull all different ways at once and it would be impossible to get anything done. He needs the freedom to choose the people he'll be working most closely with, just as Colonel Travis chose you and me as his personal assistants."

"Ha! If personal assistants were elected, I'd never have run for the position, and now I'd be free to... well, you know." That was the closest Gabrel ever came to discussing his relationship with Isovel Dayvson.

Renzi regarded his friend sympathetically. "I know this isn't what you want to be doing, Gabe. But the colonel needs us, and in any case you don't want to rush over to Harmony before the ink on the peace treaty is dry."

"I don't?"

"Give it time. There's a lot of bad feeling in Harmony about the war, and you'd be out there with no support. Better to wait until we have formal diplomatic relations and put an embassy in place. Besides," Renzi added, "if she wouldn't stay here because it would hurt her father politically, what makes you think she'll abandon him now? Let it wait."

"She just turned twenty-nine. What if she gets tired of waiting?"

Despite his complaints, Gabrel did gradually come to appreciate the great task that lay before Colonel Travis and his masterful handling of it. Elections were just the beginning of it; the new-born country needed a constitution, a legislative structure, a national bank, currency and economic policies. Judges had been appointed by the Governor-General, and the courts had been run under "Colony Law," which was an awkward hybrid of Harmony law with harsh penalties for colonists and extra control from on high added in.

"We need to do everything at once," Renzi said happily. "Rules for elections, actually hold elections and get legislators who can make Esilian law for Esilian citizens, create a court system and independent judges to administer the laws. Write a constitution, set up a national bank, fund economic development projects. Isn't it wonderful!"

In the moments between rushing through one project and wheedling the senior advisors on another project, Gabrel worried a bit about the "everything at once" part. Colonel Travis was setting the elections a year out "to give districts time to organize and select candidates." He had written an interim Constitution "to guide the nation's beginning steps." Lacking a wealthy class to invest in industrial development, he had begun allowing the national bank to fund state-owned industries. And by his direction, those industries were created in a number of underdeveloped districts, with the object of spreading economic development around the country rather than having it all centered in Colony City.

"I've heard people calling it Travis City, or just Travis," Gabriel said one night.

"And why not? Colony City was a remarkably uninspired name, not to mention being totally sucky *and* inaccurate now that we're no longer a colony. And who deserves the recognition more than Colonel Travis?"

"I'm just wondering if we aren't concentrating too much power in one man. He may be spreading out economic development, but all the political power leads back to Colonel Travis. He wrote the Constitution, he decides when elections will be held, he directs the national bank."

"He's a great man, and he's availed himself of the Reference Library in deciding all these things. What do you have against his Constitution?"

"Just that," said Gabrel. "Even you say "his" Constitution. It should be *our* Constitution – created by the people – not the work of one man."

"After the elections," Renzi said, "we'll have legislators who can draft a new Constitution, set the timing for the next elections, create a committee to supervise the national bank. All this stuff you're worrying about is just – just Duck Tape to hold things together until we can design a permanent solution."

"I expect you're right…"

* * *

But after that discussion, Gabrel abandoned all thought of going to Harmony before the first elections were held. There was talk of electing Travis as the first Prime Minister; there were suggestions that nobody else needed to bother standing for office. There was nothing Gabrel could do about it. He read history, about democracies declining into dictatorships. Esilia hadn't even *had* a democracy yet; could the first steps of the new nation lead it into a sham freedom, with a Prime Minister for life and a one-party rule? His hololetters to Isovel became short; he knew they were read by the Bureau for Security, and he did not wish to broadcast his concerns to Harmony.

Colonel Travis noticed Gabrel's new wariness. "I believe you have redefined your role in my administration."

"Indeed, sir?"

"You have taken on the burden of the slave who rides in the Emperor's carriage, whispering, 'Remember, thou art mortal.'"

Gabrel flushed. "Sir. It's not my place –"

227

"You're wrong, boy. It's every citizen's place to protect freedom. You really don't need to worry about me, though. I have no intention of standing for Prime Minister."

"The mob may not give you a choice. Sir."

"Oh, I have my plans. There is always a choice, you know."

As the temporary administration settled into place, Gabrel and Renzi had fewer emergency duties. Gabrel spent his free time reading recent history and snarling at the distortions and whitewashes produced by both sides. Someone really should write a truly impartial history of Esilia.

He wrote long letters to Isovel, which he deleted as soon as they were written, and short, carefully impersonal and apolitical messages some of which appeared to pass the censors.

Isovel's responses were also short, sometimes no more than a summary of her social calendar. To judge from the number of invitations she mentioned, General Dayvson was not exactly a political pariah in his home country. He wondered, but did not ask. Could not. Not when so many unfriendly eyes would see whatever he sent.

The clues she dropped were disheartening, to say the least.

"Wife of EduHead gave a garden party. Everybody was curious about my experiences in Esilia. A number of comments which I felt it tactful to ignore."

"Daddy very busy this week. Special meetings with friends of Andrus." *The Bureau for Security.* "They are exploring his insights into Esilian culture and asking if, as a loyal citizen, he can help them make contact with friends of Harmony over there." *They want him to help create a spy ring to prove his loyalty.* "Naturally his only desire is to serve Harmony in every possible way, but of course he knows no one in Esilia."

And finally, fatally: "The SecHead himself dined with us this week. There was a lively conversation about Daddy's experiences in Esilia, and the SecHead verified once again that he could not put them in touch with any Esilians. He made a joke out of it, saying that Daddy had been so firm in refusing that it would look very bad for him if he or any of his household was in communication with an Esilian."

That was the last time he heard from her, and the last time she accepted any messages from him.

Gabrel quit wasting time and plunged into administrative work. Three weeks later he presented Colonel Travis with a stack of detailed position papers on banking, the Esilian economy, the responsibilities of the legislature and the judiciary, and the framing of a permanent Constitution. With the papers, he submitted a formal request for leave.

Colonel Travis refused the request.

"Sir." Gabrel was desperate. "I have to go to Harmony."

"Not yet."

"We're not at war. You can't draft me. You can't force me to stay here."

"No, but Harmony can refuse to accept you, or imprison you for espionage. You have to wait until we establish diplomatic relations, boy."

"It's not up to you. I'll arrange passage on my own and make it clear that you had nothing to do with it. Your conscience will be clear."

"It will – because you're not going yet."

The only transportation between Esilia and Harmony was the same as it had been when the first exiles were landed: a steamship that took one week to make the trip. The government of Harmony had never developed aircraft that could cross the ocean, because they had no desire to make it easy for deportees to come back. And Esilia, in its years as a colony, had been forbidden to build any aircraft at all.

And the captain of the steamship informed Gabrel that Colonel Travis had already told him what to do about foolhardy young men who wanted to test the forbearance of the government on Harmony.

"I worried that he might make himself a dictator," Gabrel said to Renzi. "I should have been worrying that the people would make him a saint."

He went back to his study of history, and wasted some time writing a treatise for nobody in particular to read, comparing the Esilian war of secession with ancient separatist movements on Earth.

* * *

Harmony City, Harmony

Exactly one year after the signing of the peace treaty, and two months before the scheduled elections, the first Esilian ambassador to Harmony, accompanied by his staff and a truly impressive collection of luggage, disembarked at the port of Harmony City.

The customs officials looked longingly at the boxes and cases that the ship's men piled onto three waiting floats, but under the terms of the treaty they were not allowed to search the materials or even to inquire as to what the ambassador had considered necessary to bring with him.

The immigration official asked for names and recorded them in his personal com. It was distressingly casual, but the Bureau for Security had not contemplated the need for an immigration department until they received word that the ambassador was actually on his way. Painful as it was to admit, Harmony now shared the planet with another country on another continent, and it would be up to the Bureau to track visitors and check their passports.

Once Esilia designed passports, that is.

"I have the feeling that diplomacy is going to be as much of a learning experience as war was," one of the ambassador's aides commented, *sotto voce*, to another.

"But less fatal," the other one replied.

"Ha. Tell me that after we find out how many formal meetings we're going to suffer through."

The newly printed Esilian embassy looked as though it should still smell of wet paint, so shiny and colorful were its walls. The ambassador had issued instructions that Esilia was to emphasize its cultural differences with Harmony in every possible way. Harmony's government buildings, housing blocks, shops and private houses had all been printed as rectangular blocks in "natural" colors, meaning whatever resulted from the input material; mostly gray or mud color. The ambassador had personally paid for a license to use the newly available paint nanites, an offshoot of nanotextile development. The façade of the embassy was a brilliant blue with white details; the interior rooms all glowed with the colors of sunshine and red rock in the Esilian desert.

"Can I leave these here for now?" Gabrel jerked his head at two heavy crates which constituted most of his personal baggage.

"You would do better to leave them here permanently. By the treaty this building is Esilian soil; no citizen of Harmony may so much as look at our possessions," Colonel Travis said. "By the way – do you believe *now* that I'm not scheming to be the sole power in the Esilian government? Does my leaving the country two months before elections persuade you that I'm really not interested in becoming a dictator?"

Gabrel flushed. "I never did believe that, sir. Only – there was a time when appearances were against you."

"Bear that in mind," the colonel told him. "I think you may find that appearances are against you in the situation you're running into."

"Oh – I can deal with *appearances*," Gabrel said. "As for the books – you said they were to be a wedding present and I'm holding you to that. Get your own copy of the Reference Library for the embassy. Now, if I might – take my leave – sir?"

The colonel and Renzi watched him swing off down the street.

"He doesn't even know if she's still single, Renzi."

"She will be," Renzi said.

* * *

General Rauf Dayvson looked at the young man before him with bemusement. "It seems to be a recurring part of my life," he said. "You show up without warning and persuade me that black is white and that I can best serve my country by doing what you want."

"It only happened once before, sir. And it did serve your country."

Dayvson snorted. "And possibly saved my neck. It was touch and go when I first returned, you know. The same people who filled the streets screaming about the war came out again to shout against a peace which lost them their penal colony. There was talk of treason. But the Committee couldn't raise me up as the hero of Black Rocks and at the same time condemn me as a traitor. And very fortunately for me, the newsers convinced them that they needed a hero more than a traitor."

"You see, sir? My ideas really do work out well for everyone."

"I fail to see how your latest proposal would serve my country in any way whatsoever. But I suppose I do owe you something for the last one."

"No, well, this is – on a more personal level. If I have a position in Harmony, and a sponsor to vouch for me, I can stay here."

"*I'm* supposed to get *you* a job so you can marry my daughter? And you don't even know if she'll have you! You haven't seen or communicated with her in six months."

"How did you –"

"She told me so. Tried to make me think you two had quarreled. I didn't believe it, of course. Knew she'd broken it off for my sake, because she thought my credit couldn't survive a daughter who consorted with the enemy." Dayvson cleared his throat. "Told her not to be so stupid. Didn't get anywhere. She is a very difficult woman to manage, boy. Feel obliged to warn you."

"Ah – I don't expect to manage her, sir. I just want to marry her, and I have every expectation that she will bully me unmercifully."

"Good to think that someone can do that. I might place a few bets on the outcome, though."

The position Dayvson ultimately offered was better than anything Gabrel had dared to imagine. He cut off Gabrel's thanks with a word of advice. "You really should look at my rose garden before you go. Through the small sitting-room downstairs, there are French windows opening to the garden. I'm rather proud of it."

* * *

The roses were past their prime and badly needed cutting back to encourage new blossoms. Isovel suspected the gardener had neglected this chore because he felt it was an appropriate task for a young lady. They had only three servants – cook, gardener, and an indoor maid – which was downright spartan for the neighborhood. But three felt like a multitude when they were united on a project like Getting Miss Isovel To Do Something. She would probably have to take some appliance apart and put it back together – preferably leaving streaks of grime on the kitchen table – to convince them she wasn't terminally depressed.

Which, of course, she was *not*. One made the necessary decisions, and one moved on – chin up, and definitely not looking back. She could not split her life and her loyalties.

Also, she was not going to make a fool of herself by clinging to a much younger man in another country, who had probably found himself a nice local girlfriend by now.

So. Somehow the staff had herded her out here, with a basket and pruning shears, so they could reassure themselves by watching her do something appropriate. Isovel glowered at the blowsy, nodding pale pink blooms on *Baronne Henriette* and the hot pink petals of *Beauté Inconstante* that were beginning to drift down onto the grass. Their time was past; they had to go. Like a thirty-year-old spinster with an inappropriate fixation on an impossible young man, they had no place any more. She attacked *Baronne* first and then *Beauté* with a series of decisive snips that covered the bottom of her basket with flower heads and loose petals.

If only one could prune thoughts… and feelings… and memories in the same way. But those intangible things were harder to dispose of. Some day, the philosophers promised, she would be old and mere memories would lose their power to hurt.

She doubted that any of the philosophers had ever been a young woman who was… *not* in love. At most, *remembering* love – ridiculous that it should hurt so much.

A sound behind her. Discord! Did they have to hint her out here with her little basket and her shears and then *watch* to make sure she was behaving as they wanted? Briefly fantasizing about pruning

Daddy's prized bi-colored *Clotilde Soupert* to the roots, Isovel whirled to give the gardener a piece of her mind… and stopped, pruning shears in one hand, looking at somebody who was definitely not the gardener.

She must be losing her mind. This man couldn't really look so much like Gabrel. It was a humiliating symptom of her infatuation, thinking she caught a glimpse of Gabrel in one man's brisk stride, another's restless hands.

He walked towards her and became quite solid and three-dimensional and real – and very much himself.

"You – can't be *here*." Her throat was dry.

"I should like to convince you otherwise," Gabrel said, "but would you mind putting those shears down first? Nothing terrifies me like an angry woman with a pair of secateurs."

Then she dropped the shears, and the basket, and all the bright dying petals of *Beauté Inconstante* floated around her and carpeted the grass, and the scent of the petals bruised under their feet blended with the sharp unmistakable scent of Gabrel himself and the safety of his arms around her.

Her lips were bruised with kissing when they finally separated by a few inches, and her head was swimming with the scent of roses in the sunshine.

"Convinced now?" Gabrel asked.

"Oh, yes," Isovel murmured happily. "I don't know how you came here, and I don't care…"

He started to release her; she gave a cry of protest and put up her hands around his neck, and they melted back together. Memories, Isovel thought faintly, were nothing like so strong as she'd thought; they'd fled before the reality of Gabrel. So, apparently, had all her will power, her values, her good sense.

"Am I going to have to fight any impudent young men for you?" Gabrel murmured into the curve of her neck.

"No!" She would have been indignant if she weren't so happy.

"Good, that's simpler. I want you to come with me."

"All right."

His hands dropped to his sides and he stepped back. "Just like that? You're not going to explain to me why it's impossible for us to be together?"

Isobel thought it over for fully two seconds. "No. I tried that and it nearly killed me. I'm not – I can't do it again. Will Esilia allow me in, or are you going to smuggle me through the harbor?"

"You'll come to Esilia? No arguments?"

Away from his touch, she gained just a little coherence. "I wish it didn't have to be this way. I don't *want* to abandon Daddy, and I do worry that my desertion will be used against him. But… yes. I'll come wherever you want to go, whenever you like. I hope you can give me a little time to explain to Daddy, that's all." She grasped his shirt collar and pulled his face back to hers.

Some inarticulate, murmuring time passed before Gabrel spoke again.

"Actually, your father already knows."

"What!" That shocked her into retreating from him.

"I have, more or less, something like his blessing."

"He – agreed – to let me go to Esilia? With *you?*"

"The emphasis," Gabrel remarked, "is hardly flattering. And actually, we are not going quite so far, so perhaps you can stop worrying about your effect on your father's career."

"Well, you certainly can't stay here!"

"Oh, yes, I can. Your father is going to sponsor me for Harmony citizenship, or at least for a permanent residence permit. With a job at the university, and being married to a Citizen, he thinks it should be a mere formality."

"Job. University?" Maybe she was insane after all.

Gabrel's quick smile lit his face. "He has been eager to resume his academic work, you know. And I was able to persuade him that a junior lecturer in Esilian Affairs would bring new perspective and insights to the History Department. Apparently he has the dean under his thumb. Your father is actually quite a competent politician, you know, and doesn't need nearly as much help from his daughter as you've been imagining – and he says that the appointment is pretty much a foregone conclusion."

Isovel sank down on a conveniently placed stone bench, warm in the afternoon sun. "You already made all these plans. Before talking to me. Why did you make me think I had to choose between exile with you or Harmony and loyalty to my father?"

"I had this silly desire to know if you would choose me in spite of all the good reasons working against us."

"And if I hadn't?"

"Oh, then I would have mentioned the permanent residency and the lectureship at the university. Don't worry; I had no intention of letting you get away."

"But you thought it would be amusing to test me first!" Isovel felt a white-hot column of rage rising to her head. "How dare you, how *dare* you play your mind games with me!" She grabbed the basket and threw it at his head. Picked up the secateurs and started toward him.

Gabrel backed up so fast that he tripped and fell. "Mercy!" he cried, but he was laughing. "Not the secateurs! Anything but the secateurs!"

"And another thing!" She raged. "You lied to me from the beginning, pretending you were my age!"

Gabrel was still laughing. "I was afraid you wouldn't take me seriously. You wouldn't cut off my… nose… to spite your face, would you?"

Isovel offered her free hand to pull him up. "Never do anything like that to me again!"

"Will I have the chance?" As soon as he was standing, he slipped an arm around her waist. She fought to keep from melting against him and forgiving him immediately.

"Oh, yes. You will have *years* to demonstrate your good behavior. I'm not letting you go again."

Standing at the open French windows, Rauf Dayvson coughed gently. "I did warn him that you are a terribly managing woman, and that he'd never be able to call his soul his own, but he's still willing to take you off my hands."

"And *you!*" Isovel was still holding the secateurs, but as she brought her hand up to point at her father, Gabrel caught her wrist.

"Peace, my love. Peace. We've achieved a happy ending. Let's not waste it."

# # #